Hometown Valentine

Lissa Manley

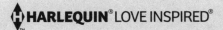

Recycling programs
for this product may
not exist in your area.

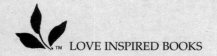 LOVE INSPIRED BOOKS

ISBN-13: 978-0-373-81818-1

Hometown Valentine

Copyright © 2015 by Melissa A. Manley

www.Harlequin.com

Printed in U.S.A.

"I need to focus on my career goals, not falling in love."

Made perfect sense, though for some reason Lily's statement had disappointment poking at him. Blake shook the emotion off. "I hear you there," he replied. "Who has time for romantic relationships?" *Or the guts.*

"Not me."

"Not me, either. I have more than I can handle with the store and Peyton."

"So you aren't interested in dating either?" she asked in what seemed like a very well-modulated voice.

"No," he said emphatically. "I don't have time." Which was part of his reasoning. The other part was too personal to share.

"Right? Me neither." She hesitated, her brow creasing. "We're actually a lot alike, you know."

"Hmm. You know, you're right."

"Maybe that's why we get along so well."

"That has to be it," he said. "We're on the same page."

"Right." She nodded. "Same page is good. Really good."

"Actually, it's excellent. We get each other."

"Yes, we do," she said, her gaze meeting his. It held. Something passed between them; what, exactly, he couldn't say, just something odd yet exciting.

Lissa Manley decided she wanted to be a published author at twelve. After she read her first romance as a teenager she decided romance was her favorite genre, although she still enjoys a good medical thriller now and then. Lissa lives in Portland, Oregon, with her husband, a grown daughter and college-aged son, and two bossy poodles. When she's not reading, she enjoys crafting, bargain hunting, cooking and decorating.

Books by Lissa Manley

Love Inspired

Moonlight Cove Series

Family to the Rescue
Mistletoe Matchmaker
Her Small-Town Sheriff
Hometown Fireman
Small-Town Homecoming
Hometown Valentine

The Heart of Main Street Series

Storybook Romance

A Snowglobe Christmas
"A Family's Christmas Wish" (novella)

Visit the Author Profile page at Harlequin.com for more titles.

Have no anxiety about anything, but in everything
by prayer and supplication with thanksgiving
let your requests be made known to God.
—*Philippians* 4:6

This book is dedicated to
my bestie and sunset sweats comrade.
Thanks for always being there for me. Tally ho!

Chapter One

Snapping her umbrella closed, Lily Rogers hurriedly stepped from the chilly late January downpour into The Coffee Cabana. The entry buzzer sounded above her head.

As the earthy smell of coffee hit her, she came to an abrupt stop just inside the door and darted her gaze around. The place was dead empty.

Odd. Washingtonians were famous for their voracious coffee appetites. She'd expected to find the place packed, especially since this store was the only thing that remotely resembled a coffee shop in Moonlight Cove.

Maybe business was bad. Lily hoped not. She desperately needed the barista job advertised in the help-wanted sign in the window. Though being a coffee jockey wasn't her dream occupation, it was a paying proposition, and those were few and far between in a town the size of her hometown. She needed money; her future as a fashion designer was at stake.

Putting her still-dripping umbrella in the metal holder by the door Lily headed toward the unmanned front counter. As she neared it, she heard a shrill sound that seemed to be coming from behind a door to the left of the counter. She cocked her head, her eyebrows drawn together. Was that a…baby crying?

She listened intently. Yes, yes, it was. The sound was a baby wailing, actually. Her well-developed baby-soothing instincts had her immediately cringing. Her youngest sister, Laura, had shrieked like that from dawn to dusk when she'd been a newborn.

Lily stood there for a moment, unsure of what to do. Was the place even open? The door had been unlocked, and it was the middle of normal business hours on a Monday, so she assumed so. Should she go look for the manager? Just leave a résumé on the counter? Hunt for the shrieking infant? What? She hadn't planned on finding the place deserted, and she certainly hadn't expected to encounter an unseen child in distress.

Just as she was about to go find the baby and take care of the poor thing, the door behind the counter opened and a man holding said screaming infant over his broad shoulder stepped out.

Ah. One mystery solved.

The man, who appeared to be around Lily's age of thirty, give or take, moved toward her. As the grayish light from the windows hit his face, she realized that everything about him screamed exhaustion. Mussed hair. Dark shadows under his eyes. Sagging shoulders. Clearly this baby had been on a crying jag of epic proportions. Lily knew how grueling that could be.

As he drew closer, she took a moment to surreptitiously study him, noting that the mussed hair was dark, thick and wavy. Touchable. The obvious shadows under his eyes did nothing to detract from the beauty of their clear, sky-blue color. And though his whole upper body hung heavy with obvious fatigue, he had the physique of an athlete. Or gym rat. Whatever. He was definitely the best-looking haggard guy she'd ever seen.

"May I help you?" he asked loudly. Tiredly. Judging by the way the baby was kicking its legs, it was one unhappy camper.

"Um...well, yes." She adjusted the strap of the pleather briefcase she'd bought at a thrift store in Pacific Beach on her shoulder and tried to tune out the baby's piercing cries. Or at the very least ignore them as best she could, despite her nurturing instincts hovering on high alert. "I'm looking for the manager."

"That would be me. I'm Blake Stonely." He yawned, putting his free hand over his mouth. "Sorry."

"Oh, okay," she said at full volume. "I'm Lily Rogers, and I wanted to apply for the job."

"The job?" He jiggled the baby, then started awkwardly rocking from foot to foot. "Oh, man, did I leave the sign out?"

Disappointment dug in. *No job?* "Yes, it's there." She'd seen it as she'd dashed through the rain from her mom's car to the front door.

"I'm so sorry, the job's been filled, just an hour ago, actually."

Lily clenched her jaw. She was a mere hour too late? Great. Just great.

Blake jostled the baby. "What with Peyton here crying up a storm, I forgot to remove the sign."

As if in reaction to her—or his—name, Peyton's staccato cries grew louder. Harsher. More frantic.

Lily's heart just about shattered, which helped take her mind off, at least temporarily, the fact that her one and only job lead had dried up, just like that.

"This has been going on since 5:00 a.m.,"

he muttered, his voice coated in bone-tired exhaustion. "And she only slept three hours last night."

Ah. A little girl. "Oh, that's rough." Lily wanted to ask where Peyton's mom was, but she held back. Clearly he was on his own with the baby, at least for the moment.

Without thinking much, she lifted up her arms. "Mind if I try?" Many years spent helping her mom with her four younger siblings—Laura in particular—might help Peyton to settle down. Besides, the crying was pitiful and really tugged on Lily's heartstrings.

He raised his brows. "You want to try getting her to stop crying?"

"Yes, I would." She waggled her hands. "Hand her over. Besides, you look like you need a break." As in, he looked like death warmed over. Twice. Not that she'd say that. He clearly had his hands full.

"O-okay," he said, holding the baby out, then turning her to face Lily. "But nothing works." In seeming response, Peyton kicked her little legs and screamed louder.

Lily took Peyton from him, noting her red, scrunched-up, tear-stained face. "Hey, little girl." Lily recalled what had worked with her middle sister, Lydia, and gently laid Peyton back in the crook of her elbow while her other arm slid under Peyton's bottom. "What seems to be the problem?"

Peyton paused for a moment, staring up at Lily with clear blue eyes that looked a lot like her daddy's. Blessed silence engulfed the room.

Lily was certain the quiet was just temporary.

Sure enough, after a few beats of silence, Peyton started up again, going stiff and screwing up her face and letting loose with a wail that pierced Lily's ears.

Blake held out his hands, a look of pure defeat on his face. "See? I told you."

"Give me a moment." With well-practiced precision she began to smoothly swing Peyton from side to side, maintaining eye contact. Automatically, Lily began to sing a lullaby in a hushed voice as she walked away from the counter—swing, swing, swing—back and forth from side to side in wide arcs, smooth as silk.

Peyton still cried, squirming, her little body tense. But after Lily's third circuit around the small space, weaving in and out of the tables, the baby's cries grew less frantic. Lily kept moving—swing, swing, swing—and by the time she made her way back to Blake, who'd slumped exhaustedly into a chair by the counter, Peyton had quieted and was drifting off to sleep.

Blake gave Lily an incredulous look, then opened his mouth to talk.

Lily shook her head and kept singing.

Rising, he pointed to the door from which he'd emerged earlier. She nodded and followed him into a small room that was obviously his office-slash-makeshift nursery. The space had a large, neat desk and task chair facing out from one corner, one other beat-up plastic chair opposite the desk and a rickety-looking bookcase with a well-organized collection of books and folders in the other corner. The rest of the area was taken up by a playpen and numerous other items of baby paraphernalia, all neatly arranged in one corner. A literal stockpile of kid equipment.

He turned and indicated the playpen, which was lined in all kinds of fleecy blankets, showing Lily she should put Peyton down there. But Lily was no baby care rookie; it was always wise to hold on to a baby for a few minutes to be sure she was actually sound asleep. She held up a finger—*Wait…*

Blake gestured in acknowledgment and then went over and plopped into the desk chair, his shoulders sagging. He ran a hand over his head, and suddenly it was obvious why his hair was so messy. She was surprised he had any left. Clearly he'd had a rough go lately.

She kept swinging Peyton, back and forth in a comforting motion. Pretty soon every muscle in her little body went limp and Lily knew the baby slept soundly enough to be put down. Ever so carefully she bent over, holding her breath, and laid Peyton on her back amid the blankets, pulling one up to cover her, snug and warm. Lily waited, hoping Peyton had worn herself out and would sleep, as much for her own sake as Blake's.

Peyton slept on, even as Lily rose and pointed to the door. She went out into the store and Blake followed her, closing the door quietly behind him.

"You're amazing," he said when they were away from the door. "She hasn't gone down for a decent nap in days."

His praise warmed her up inside. "I just have lots of experience with babies."

His eyebrows rose. "You have kids?"

"Goodness, no." Kids tied a person down, limited their options. "I'm the oldest of four younger siblings and I helped raise them." As the oldest girl it had fallen upon Lily to supply child care so Mom could work cleaning houses and at the local grocery store to keep the household afloat.

"Ah, I see," Blake said. "Well, I appreciate your help. I've been at my wit's end trying to get her to sleep."

Curiosity rose in Lily, and she wanted to ask about Peyton's mom. She opened her mouth to voice her question, but she clamped it shut just as quickly. She didn't want to pry or bring up a possibly sensitive subject. She barely knew this man.

"You're probably wondering about Peyton and me." He put a green apron on.

Lily canted her head slightly. "Kind of." Dying to know, actually.

"Peyton is my niece." He filled a sink behind the counter with water, his jaw visibly tight. "My sister was her mother."

Was? Lily's heart sank. This didn't sound good. She said nothing and simply waited for him to go on.

"She...um..." He turned the water off and stood with his head down and his eyes closed, clearly composing himself.

Lily's eyes burned.

Finally he went on. "She was killed by a drunk driver a month ago, and I have temporary custody of Peyton."

"Oh, no." She swiped at tears that had sprung up. "I'm so sorry."

"Thanks."

"What about Peyton's father?" she asked, then realized she was being nosy.

"He and Anna weren't married, but were planning a wedding next summer," he replied in an even tone. "He was killed in the line of duty in Afghanistan while Anna was pregnant."

A knot formed in Lily's chest. "Oh, no. So she's an orphan. Poor little thing. Thankfully she has you."

"Anna and I were very close, and losing her...well, it's been really rough."

Empathy welled. "I'm sure it has." Suddenly, his story tweaked a memory. "Did the accident happen out on Old Pass Road?"

He just nodded ever so slightly, seemingly incapable of speech.

"I used to work at The Clothes Horse, and Jean, the owner of the store, mentioned that accident." Jean had suddenly decided to retire and close the store last week. Hence, Lily's need for a job.

"Yeah, that was Anna," he said, his voice husky. "Peyton was only three months old when her mom died."

A horrific thought occurred to Lily. "Was the baby in the car?"

"Thankfully, no. Peyton was with me. Anna was on her way to a doctor's appointment in

Pacific Beach, and was in the wrong place at the wrong time." He let out a shaky sigh. "She was only supposed to be gone for an hour or two."

Lily shook her head. "I'm so sorry. I know how rough it is to lose someone you love."

He looked at her, his gaze questioning.

"My dad died of cancer when I was in high school, and though my grief has muted over time, I still miss him terribly." Everything had changed that day. Lily's life most of all. Mom had gone to work, and Lily had become her younger siblings' primary caretaker. All of her dreams had been deferred then.

"So the grief gets better?" Blake asked, a twinge of hope in his voice.

"Yes, it does." It had taken a while to ease— a long while, actually—but Lily didn't want to depress him even more.

"I hope so." He turned the water back on and squirted some soap in the sink.

Lily looked around. "So, you're running the business and taking care of Peyton full-time?"

"I usually have help with Peyton, but my babysitter called in sick yesterday. Hopefully she'll be back tomorrow."

"You've got a lot on your plate."

"Yes, I do." He put some dishes in the sink

and turned the water off. "I had no idea what goes into parenting."

"It's a full-time job." One Lily didn't want for a long while. She was determined not to follow in her mother's footsteps. No kids, no man, nothing tying her down right now. Now that her sister Laura was close to graduating from high school, Lily finally had the opportunity to pursue her own dream of winning the TV show *Project Fashion* and becoming a fashion designer.

"And I already have one running this place, so I've been crazy busy." Blake gestured around. "I haven't even had time to do my morning routine."

"But the job is taken?" she asked, going back to the reason she was here. She'd saved every penny she'd made working part-time at The Clothes Horse, except for what she'd given Mom for unexpected car repairs, but Lily was still several thousand dollars short if she were to save for the plane fare and rent in LA, where she planned on staying indefinitely. A temporary job until June was a must.

"Yes, I'm sorry, it is." Blake headed out toward the tables. "A kid showed up midmorning and I hired him." He gathered a few empty coffee cups. "He starts tomorrow."

Disappointment clogged Lily's throat. "The early bird gets the worm, right?"

"Yeah, I guess that's true." Blake frowned. "Again, I'm sorry."

"Not your fault." She should have come in yesterday when she'd first seen the sign. But Laura had needed a ride to basketball practice, and with Mom at work, Lily had had to take her. Seemed there was always something pulling at her these days.

He dried off his hands on a bar towel, then went to the register and grabbed a pen and a pad of paper. "Here, write your name down and if the kid doesn't work out, I'll call you."

She did so, then handed him the paper. "Thanks. I'd appreciate it."

"And I appreciate your help with Peyton."

"No problem. She's a darling little girl."

His blue eyes went soft. "Yes, she is. Now, if I could just get her to be a quiet little girl, we'd be golden."

"It'll get better." Lily held her arms as if she were holding a baby, then did the baby-soothing swing, swing, swing. "And remember the motion."

He nodded. "Right. I'll give your technique a try."

"If you need any more help, you know how

to reach me. Call me anytime." Belatedly she realized that her comment could have been construed as an invitation to ask her out. "For baby advice," she said in a remarkably even voice. Yeah, just that. She definitely wasn't looking for any kind of romance. She remembered how broken Mom had been after Daddy died. Lily never wanted to be so vulnerable to emotional devastation by a man. And, anyway, she was determined to leave Moonlight Cove permanently and follow her own dreams in LA.

"I hope I can keep track of your number," he said. "Sleep deprivation has made me spacey."

"I know how that can be. My mom routinely lost track of what day it was when she was up all night with babies. My twin brothers just about drove her around the bend." Liam and Larry were still wild, though they were both now in college. Funny how they'd escaped to follow their dreams and Lily hadn't. The benefit of being male and not firstborn in her family.

A look of horror materialized on Blake's face. "I can't imagine having two at once."

"Well, by that time I was old enough to help out quite a bit, which made things a bit easier." For Mom. Not so much for Lily.

"How old were you when they were born?"

"Nine. And then she had two more after them."

He paused, clearly doing the math in his head. "So…that's five kids?"

"Yep. My youngest sister, Laura, is a senior in high school."

"Wow. Five." He shook his head. "I can barely handle one."

"Well, the twins are now in college, so we lived."

The buzzer sounded, signaling the arrival of a customer. Lily turned and saw Mrs. De Marco, one of her mom's cleaning clients, enter the store. Mrs. De Marco was clad in a sturdy-looking raincoat, and had a plastic rain hat covering her silver-gray hair. She carried several shopping bags in her gnarled hands.

Lily rushed forward. "Here, Mrs. De Marco, let me help you with those."

"Oh, bless you, Lily." She handed one of the bags over. "I thought I could handle them, but as usual, I've overestimated my ability to actually be able to get my treasures to my car."

Lily put one bag on a nearby table, then took the other one from Mrs. De Marco. "No problem. I'm strong."

"You take after your mother, then," Mrs.

De Marco said, removing her rain hat. "She's a hard worker and does a wonderful job cleaning my house. Even the hard jobs like scrubbing floors."

Lily put the other bag down, wondering what Mrs. De Marco had purchased. Bricks, maybe? "Yes, she definitely works hard." A widow with five kids had little choice.

Mrs. De Marco toddled to the counter. "Well, hello, young man."

Blake inclined his head. "Good afternoon, Mrs. De Marco. Your usual?"

"Yes, please."

"Double low-fat latte, heavy on the whipped cream and caramel, coming right up." Blake went to work behind the counter.

Lily stepped back to stand beside Mrs. De Marco. "Why don't I help you get your bags to your car?"

"Oh, dear, would you?"

"Of course."

"That would be wonderful. With this rain, my packages would be soaked by the time I managed to get them in the trunk."

"Would you like some coffee?" Blake asked Lily.

"Oh, no, I'm fine," Lily replied. Actually, a warm drink sounded good, but coffee drinks weren't in her budget.

"Oh, pshaw," Mrs. De Marco said, waving a hand. "It's cold and rainy out. You need something to warm you up."

Lily shook her head. "No, it's fine, really."

"Well, I'm getting you a drink, on me."

"I don't know…" Lily said. Her mother had instilled in her a strong desire to provide for herself.

"I insist, my dear." Mrs. De Marco looked at Blake. "She'll have what I'm having, to go, of course."

Lily gave up the fight. Clearly Mrs. De Marco had it in her head to treat Lily to coffee. And, actually, a steamy, rich coffee concoction sounded lovely; she couldn't remember the last time she'd had a store-bought drink, much less one with whipped cream on top. How decadent!

Mrs. De Marco paid, and then she and Lily sat at a nearby table. While they waited for their drinks, Lily did her best not to stare at Blake as he worked with quiet efficiency behind the counter making the coffees.

The more she saw him in action, though, the more she decided he was one of the best-looking men she'd ever seen. Something about the combination of his dark hair and blue eyes, maybe? Or perhaps it was his broad shoulders and lean waist? Or maybe his sculpted cheeks and firm jawline, which, she'd noticed, was whisker-shadowed in the most appealing way? Add to that the fact that he'd taken in his orphaned niece and was willingly raising her, and yes, he was definitely attractive.

"Lily, dear, our drinks are ready," Mrs. De Marco said as she stood. "This weather has made my hip cranky, and now that I've sat down, I'd just as soon wait by the door. Would you mind getting them?"

"Oh, um, yes," Lily said, thankful Mrs. De Marco had pulled Lily's thoughts away from the owner of the store. She went over to the front counter to pick up their drinks, very studiously keeping her gaze off Blake. Nothing but trouble there. She needed to get out of there.

Just as her hands touched the drinks and she was about to make her getaway, he caught her eye with a wave and lift of his chin.

She stopped, her hands falling to her sides, her heart giving a little hiccup.

He came over, a towel slung across one broad shoulder. "Thank you so much for your help with Peyton today," he said, a light smile gracing his face, magically transforming him from haggardly handsome to flat-out drop-dead gorgeous.

Wow. As if he needed to get any better looking.

He went on. "Even a little break was great, and I'll definitely be using your swing technique."

She swallowed and tried not to gawk. "You're welcome," she managed, somehow sounding completely unaffected by him. When had she become such a good fake-out artist?

Blake flipped the towel down and began wiping the counter in front of her, bending just a tad closer. "Again, if the kid I hired doesn't work out, I'll call."

She picked up the drinks, glad they had lids. "Okay, sounds great." She lifted one drink-laden hand. "Bye."

With that she turned and headed to the front door, where Mrs. De Marco waited, sure she would never hear from Blake Stonely ever again.

And given her unwanted reaction to him, that was probably for the best.

Blake covertly watched Lily and Mrs. De Marco as they walked away. After a brief discussion, Lily grabbed her umbrella from the holder by the door with her free hand and then followed Mrs. De Marco out. Before the door could even close, Lily had the umbrella up and over the elderly woman to keep her from getting wet.

Blake watched them walk left, presumably toward Mrs. De Marco's car. He couldn't help but be impressed by Lily Rogers. She'd jumped in to help him out, and had also been quick in assisting Mrs. De Marco. He liked her. From afar, of course. And there was no harm in that.

Once the ladies were out of view, he turned and began putting clean coffee mugs in their place. But his thoughts remained on Lily. She'd looked younger than his own age of thirty-one, but she had to be close to that age to have brothers in college who were nine years younger than she. He'd noticed that she was tall and slender with long chestnut-hued hair and a pale, smooth complexion devoid of much makeup. Very pretty, in a natural, girl-next-door kind of way.

What a refreshing change after Amy, who'd spent a good hour in the morning getting ready for work and was always shopping for the latest makeup products and clothes in Manhattan, where they'd both lived and worked. He'd guess she spent a good portion of her lawyer's paycheck on makeup, her expensive car and clothes every month.

Just the thought of his former fiancée had Blake's hackles rising. He let out a breath, searching for calm. Had he really lived that high-flying lifestyle once? It seemed five life-times ago, though in reality he'd left New York just under a year and a half ago.

Left New York. The burn of failure spread through him, hollowing out his gut as it always did. He couldn't bomb out again.

He looked around The Cabana and his re-solve wavered. Though he'd had a spurt of cus-tomers this morning, overall business wasn't good and the shop was hovering on the edge of red. And now with Peyton to take care of, he was wondering how he was going to make it all work.

How was he going to keep the wolf away this time?

Just the thought of failing again filled him with dread, and made him wonder if he'd done the right thing by following Anna to Moon-light Cove when his job had gone bust in New York. It had seemed like the perfect plan to Blake: move to Moonlight Cove, live in the same town with Jim and Fran, and Anna, too, who had moved to Moonlight Cove three years earlier to be close to Jim and Fran, as well. His family. Small but perfect.

But now Anna was gone.

A wave of grief washed over him and he felt his eyes burn.

His downward spiral of emotions was interrupted when the buzzer over the door rang, signaling the arrival of a customer. Blake looked up.

A group of five ladies he didn't recognize—tourists, he figured—came in and ordered, keeping his hands busy for the next little while, and his mind focused on the here and now.

Just as they all sat at a table by the window, drinks in hand, two more customers came in. He recognized Jeb Campbell, who ran the local hardware store, and Myra Fleming, the local librarian. He got them their drinks, and very quickly the bell over the door was going off again. Maybe all this business was a sign of busy times to come.

Blake looked up from making a fresh pot of brew and saw Jim Wilson, his foster father, come in, his trademark baseball cap in his hands—he'd always been a stickler for manners. Jim's gray hair was, as usual, cut military short and neat. He wore a pair of worn jeans and a green windbreaker, and had a large square bandage on his right cheek. Jim was in treatment for a relapse of skin cancer and had just had a biopsy yesterday. Just the thought of losing someone else filled Blake with heart-rending grief.

"Hey. What are you doing up and about?" Blake said as Jim headed to the counter. "I know for a fact you're supposed to be resting."

"Aw, don't you start," Jim said, waving a hand. "Fran's been all over me to take it easy, and she knows I hate just lyin' around." Fran was Jim's wife of forty years and one of the most wonderful, kindhearted women Blake knew. He'd been blessed with fantastic foster parents. Having no kids of their own, Fran and Jim, Blake's freshman math teacher, had taken Blake and Anna in out of the goodness of their very big hearts when Blake and Anna's mom had died of a drug overdose during Blake's freshman year. Blake and Anna's dad had walked out when Anna was just a few months old.

"That's because she cares about you, and because you're a stubborn old goat when it comes to taking care of yourself."

"I know. I just needed some fresh air, so I thought I'd come down here and get me a cup of your strongest brew."

"Coming right up." Blake turned and went to the special pot of straight black coffee he kept just for all of the older customers who weren't interested in frothy drinks and just wanted a good old-fashioned cup of hot joe. He poured, expecting to see sludge ooze out at any moment. To each his own.

He set the cup of goo in front of Jim.

As usual, Jim went for his wallet.

"It's on the house," Blake said per tradition, waiting for the dialogue that always followed.

"You sure?"

"I'm sure," Blake said, taking comfort in the reliability of their discussion.

"If you insist."

"I do."

"Okay, then." Jim picked up the cup and drank. He sighed heavily. "Oh, yeah, just what I needed on such a wet, cold day, especially since Fran only serves decaf."

"You still telling her that's what I always give you?"

"Maybe," Jim said with a quirk of his lips.

"If she asks me, I'll tell the truth." Blake's mom had lied to him and Anna all the time about anything and everything; he hated false-hoods, even harmless ones.

"I'd expect nothing less." Jim looked around. "Place seems busy."

"Right now," Blake replied, his jaw tight. Jim knew the business was struggling. Though

The Coffee Cabana was the only stand-alone coffee store in town, for some reason the locals weren't coming in as much as Blake had planned. He did okay in the summer, when the tourist business was good. But it wasn't enough to sustain the business all year.

"Overall, though?" Jim asked, his blue eyes intent.

"Still not good." Blake swung around and turned on the sink's faucet.

"My offer is still open."

"I'm not taking your money." Jim had offered a loan a few months ago, and Blake had turned him down then. "You've already done enough for me." Saved his and Anna's lives, actually. He couldn't ask for anything more from him and Fran.

"You're determined to make this place work on your own, aren't you?" Jim asked, his hands hugging his coffee cup.

"Yes, I am." Blake turned off the faucet. "I failed once. I'm not letting it happen a second time."

"I know, I know." Jim nodded. "I was just hoping that maybe you'd reconsider, especially now that you've got Peyton to think about."

Blake set his hands on the counter and leaned in. "It's been a challenge, handling her and the store, but I'm going to make it work."

What other choice did he have? He had to do right by Anna and take care of Peyton, and letting go of The Cabana was out of the question.

"You sure you don't want me and Fran to pitch in?"

"You're on medical leave fighting cancer, and Fran works full-time." Fran was a bookkeeper for a local business. "I can't impose on you."

"I guess I was just thinking when you moved here we'd be able to help out more."

"You have helped out, more than anybody else has ever helped me." Blake went over to the bakery case and grabbed a marionberry muffin, Jim's favorite, then went back to the counter. "But I have to do this by myself to prove I can succeed on my own." He pulled a plate out from an undercounter shelf, put the muffin on it and set it down in front of Jim. He just stared at Jim, one eyebrow raised, daring him to try to pay for it.

"I know, but we'd still like to jump in however we can."

"Not necessary."

Without saying a word, Jim peeled off the paper liner and took a bite. When he was done chewing, he looked at Blake. "Are you ever going to forgive yourself for what happened in New York?"

"I made a bad call and not only lost all I'd worked so hard for, I also lost some of my clients' money." Blake drew in a steadying breath, trying to breathe around the lump forming in his throat. "I'm not sure that's something I'm ever going to be okay with." Getting that pink slip had been the bitter icing on the cake.

"You have to forgive yourself before you can move on," Jim said, his eyes full of empathy.

"I know," Blake said. This wasn't the first time he and Jim had had this conversation. "And that sounds easy." Deceptively so.

"But it isn't."

"Right." Blake had thought rebounding from the debacle of his life in New York would be the most difficult thing he'd ever have to do. Now he realized trying to run a business while being responsible for a baby would hold that place of distinction in his life. Funny how things could turn on a dime.

Jim looked at him over his coffee cup, then put the mug on the counter. "Say, I saw Lily Rogers and Maria De Marco a block up a few minutes ago with to-go cups in their hands."

"Yes, they were here," Blake replied.

"I had all of Lily's siblings in my math class." Jim had taught freshman math at Moonlight Cove High School since he and Fran had moved here ten years ago to be closer to Fran's ailing mother. "Liam, Larry, Lydia and Laura. All *L*s."

"She was here applying for the job."

"Ah," Jim said, wiping his hands. "Did you hire her?"

"No, I already found someone and hired him." Blake rubbed at a spot on the counter. "He starts tomorrow."

"Oh, well, good. Sounds like you have it all worked out," Jim said.

Right as Jim finished speaking, Jay Wright, the local insurance agent, came in and headed straight for the front counter. He ordered, and as soon as Blake was finished serving him he went back over to Jim.

"Lily came to a couple of Liam and Larry's parent conferences. She's a very nice young woman," Jim said without preamble.

"Yes, she is." One of the nicest Blake had met here in Moonlight Cove. Not that he'd met many; he didn't have a lot of time for any kind of social life.

"I'm pretty sure she's single," Jim said, looking over his coffee cup with a speculative gaze. "At least the last I heard."

Blake deadpanned him.

"What?" Jim said, shrugging. "You're single. She's single. In my day, guys took note of that kind of stuff. And we asked nice young women out on dates."

"You know I'm not interested in dating," Blake said. "And you know why."

"Just because Amy was unfeeling and greedy doesn't mean all women are like that."

"She dumped me when I lost most of my money," Blake said, the words bitter on his tongue. Though he knew now he hadn't really loved Amy, she had mortally wounded his pride when she'd dumped him, and a wall had gone up around his heart.

"So, what? You plan on being alone for the rest of your life?" Jim asked with a lift of his grizzled brow.

"Between that and my business problems and now Peyton, dating is the last thing on my mind." Seems he'd spent his life being abandoned by women. Even when she was alive, Mom hadn't been there for him or Anna. Essentially killing herself with drugs had been the final blow. No way was he taking another chance.

"Fair enough," Jim said, canting his head and nodding. "But nice, attractive, kind women aren't always easy to come by. Maybe you should keep an eye on Lily Rogers, just in case you change your mind."

The overhead bell rang, and the lovely subject of their conversation came sailing back into the store, her windswept, damp hair fluffed up around her rosy cheeks.

Blake watched her, his heartbeat accelerating just a bit.

She pointed to the floor next to the chair she'd been sitting in. "I forgot my briefcase," she said embarrassedly. Bending down, she picked it up and slung it over her slim shoulder. "Sometimes I wonder where my brain is." She pointed to her head and made a silly expression.

Blake found himself smiling.

Like a pretty whirlwind of constant motion she headed back to the door and with another wave she was gone into the rain-swept afternoon as quickly as she'd reappeared.

Still grinning, Blake turned his attention to Jim. "More coffee?"

Jim shook his head and placed his hand over his cup. "So, the way you tell it, you're not interested in Lily."

"Yes, that's right," Blake said, infusing an extra amount of certainty into his voice. He had to head this off or Jim would have Blake and Lily on a date this very night and head over heels in love by the weekend. Jim was a hopeless romantic, and fully prescribed to the love-conquers-all theory of life.

Blake thought that attitude was shortsighted and idealistic. Real life had taught him to be wary of letting others gain control of one's heart.

"Then why were you watching her so intently just now?" Jim asked, his blue eyes trained on Blake like a laser.

Blake's face heated. Caught. Worse yet, he didn't have a plausible response. So he just glared at Jim.

Jim chuckled. "That's what I thought," he said with a twinkle in his eyes. "You like Lily, my friend. More than you think you should."

Blake was very afraid Jim was right.

No matter. He'd probably never see her again.

Chapter Two

Blake rang the doorbell of Molly and Grant Roderick's house, holding Peyton's baby carrier in his right hand. It felt odd to be arriving at a social function when his focus for the past month had been on the store and Peyton and nothing else remotely resembling any kind of life. But he needed some kind of social interaction, some kind of break, or he'd lose it. Though he was only acquainted with Grant and Molly as customers at The Cabana, and the one time Blake had come to a singles' group function had been about a year ago, he was still grateful to them for including him.

The door opened and Grant stood there. "Hey, Blake. Glad you could make it." With a welcoming smile, he moved back and gestured Blake in.

"Thanks." Blake stepped through the threshold into an oak-trimmed entryway and set the carrier on the floor. "I appreciate you letting me bring the baby."

Grant bent down and looked at a bundled-up, sleeping Peyton, smiling. "No problem at all. We all love babies. And it's good for you to have a break from your killer schedule."

Blake unbuttoned his coat. "Yeah, it's been a little rough." Peyton had slept a little better last night, but had still woken up fussing three times. And Mrs. Jones was still sick, so he'd had to juggle Peyton and the store again today. He really hoped Mrs. Jones was able to work tomorrow; another day doing double duty wouldn't be good, even though the kid he'd hired as a barista, Jonah, was doing well. Blake was already behind in never-ending paperwork and the general administrative tasks inherent in owning a business. "Thanks." He took his coat off and put it in Grant's outstretched hand.

"I know I've said it before, but I'm so sorry about Anna." Grant opened a nearby closet and hung up Blake's coat.

A lump formed in Blake's chest. "Thanks." If he said more, he'd probably break down, so he left it at that.

"Everybody's in the kitchen, so right this way," Grant said, gesturing behind himself.

Blake picked up Peyton and followed Grant

through a good-size living room tastefully decorated with brown leather couches, a colorful area rug, a large-screen TV and two dog beds sitting side by side. Voices floated to him from the kitchen.

When he stepped into the room, several heads turned. He recognized Molly, and a few other people who'd been into the store, though he didn't know their names.

Molly stepped forward from the family room adjoining the kitchen, drawing his attention. "Blake! It's good to see you."

"Thanks for having me." He saw the snack spread on the table and mentally slapped his head. "Oh, I guess I should have brought something."

She waved a hand. "No worries." Her gaze went to Peyton. "You have this little angel to take care of." Molly bent over. "She's adorable."

"Thanks." Thankfully, Peyton slept on, even with the conversation in the room. Figured that *now* she would sleep. "Still. I should have realized it was a potluck." Where was his brain lately? Lost in the haze of sleep deprivation and overwork, probably.

"Do you want to bring her with you while I introduce you around?" Molly asked.

"You want me to take her?" a familiar female voice asked from behind him.

He turned, and there stood Lily Rogers, a lovely smile on her face. "Hey!" he said, surprised to see her here. She wore a blue-and-white-striped top and had her hair up on top of her head, showing off her slender neck. Wow. She was even prettier than he remembered.

"Hey back," she said, her eyes catching on his for just a moment before shifting to focus on Peyton. "How's my girl Peyton these days?"

"Quieter," he replied drily. "At least for now."

"Oh, good."

"I understand you and Lily met yesterday," Molly said.

"Yes, she came in to apply for a job," he said.

"How's the new guy working out?" Lily asked.

"He's fine," Blake said. "Fortunately he had barista experience, so I haven't had to do too much training."

"I'll have to come in and hit him with some random, weird order," Lily said. "Put him through his paces."

"Go for it," Blake replied, liking the levity she brought to the conversation, even though she was discussing a job she hadn't gotten.

Lily held her hand out. "Why don't I take

her into the living room, where it's quiet, while you relax for a bit."

"You sure you don't mind?" He didn't come here to foist Peyton off on someone else; he knew where his responsibilities lay.

"Of course not," Lily replied, shooing him away. "Go meet everyone."

"You'll let me know if you need me?"

"I can handle her if she fusses," Lily said with a crooked smile.

The teasing glint in Lily's eyes made his heart bounce. "Yes, I guess you can." Smiling back, he handed her the carrier. "Here you go."

She hoisted it into the crook of her arm and headed into the living room. He couldn't help but notice the curls at her nape as she walked away.

Grant came up and handed him a glass of what looked like lemonade. "You know Lily?"

"She came in yesterday to apply for the barista job." Blake took a sip of his drink. Tart, but good. "I had to tell her it was already filled."

"She seems to like Peyton," Molly observed.

"She helped out yesterday when it got busy and Peyton was having a fit." He smiled. "She's a genuine baby whisperer."

"She's also a very good clothing designer." Grant looked at Molly. "Didn't you tell me she wants to go to LA and audition for some fashion reality show?"

"Yes, *Project Fashion*," Molly said. "She's very talented. She designs and makes most of her own clothes."

Surprise and unexpected disappointment washed through Blake. "She didn't mention any of this yesterday."

"Going to the audition has been in the works for a while."

"I got the impression she helped with her brothers and sisters a lot." Her commitment to her family had impressed Blake yesterday.

"Yes, her dad died when she was in her early teens and Lily has helped her mom with her siblings since then." Molly put her arm around Grant's waist. "She's put off her own dream for her family. She lost her job at a local clothing store last week, so she really needs one." Molly waved at someone who'd just stepped into the kitchen. "She helps her mom out with bills and stuff, so it's taken her a long time to save the money she needs to go to LA."

More admiration spread through Blake. "I wish I could have hired her, then. Even temporarily."

"Hopefully she'll find something else soon," Molly said.

"Sounds like she's pretty set on the reality

show," Blake replied, still feeling inexplicably disappointed Lily would eventually be leaving town.

"Oh, she is," Molly said, nodding. "I think she could win, too, if she just had the chance. Either way she plans on staying in LA for the foreseeable future."

Blake suddenly heard Peyton crying. "Excuse me," he said. "Peyton calls."

He headed into the living room, and there sat Lily, holding a screeching Peyton. "Hey, there," he said, rushing over. "What's up?"

Lily stood, pulling Peyton close so her head was touching Lily's cheek. "She just started in." Her face froze. "Oh, wow. I think she has a fever."

With concern bubbling through him, Blake laid a hand on Peyton's forehead. Though he was no nurse, even he could tell she was way too hot to the touch. "I think you're right."

"Poor baby," Lily said.

He leaned in to look at Peyton's flushed face, trying to ignore how close he was to Lily. "She's never been sick before," he said as more worry chomped away at him.

"All babies eventually get sick." Lily pulled away slightly and then started in with the swing, swing, swing thing she did so well. She gave him a look tinged in sympathy. "Not that that makes it any easier."

Peyton quieted just a bit.

"I have no idea what to do with a sick kid," he said, swiping a hand through his hair. He was so out of his element trying to take care of Peyton.

"Infant fever reducer would be a start."

"Do I just get that at the grocery store?" This fatherhood thing was complicated.

"Yep," Lily said. "It's in the pain reliever section."

He scratched his cheek. "How do I give her a pill?"

"It's a liquid you can put in her formula, or squeeze in her mouth with a dropper."

"Oh, okay." There was so much to learn. He stood for a moment, his shoulders sagging. He was just barely keeping his head above water; how was he going to handle the store and a sick baby? He prayed Mrs. Jones would be back at work tomorrow. If not…was it possible Lily could help him out? She did need a job. Hopefully he wouldn't have to ask, but he filed the idea away, just in case.

"I know it's scary to have her be sick, but since she's too young to be teething, it's probably just a virus that will go away in a few days."

He let out a heavy breath. "I hope so."

Peyton started wailing again.

Molly came into the room, her brow creased. "Is everything okay?"

"Peyton has a fever," he said. "I should go." He rubbed Peyton's overly warm head. "I don't want to spread germs around."

"Once you get the medicine in, she'll feel a lot better," Lily said. "She'll probably conk out as soon as you get home."

"I hope so," he said. Just the thought of another sleepless night filled him with dread. Of course, he'd do whatever she needed. But the strain of no sleep and another long day tomorrow made him feel as if he wore a cement coat.

As Lily tried to put Peyton back in the carrier, the baby arched her back and screamed, making it difficult for Lily to get the straps over her head.

More worry scraped across Blake's nerves.

"I know, sweetie," Lily soothed as she got the Y strap over Peyton's head and snapped it in. "Daddy needs to get you home."

"I'm so sorry you have to leave," Molly said, handing Lily Peyton's blanket. "You'll have to come to next month's get-together."

He just nodded. Though he'd given the gathering tonight a try, at this point, with so many things pulling on him, socializing had fallen to last on his list. Maybe he'd feel like going out…in a million years or so. Or maybe when Peyton turned eighteen. Provided she was still with him then. Permanent custody still hadn't been determined yet.

Lily tucked the blanket around Peyton and stepped back. "There you go. Nice and cozy."

Blake picked up the carrier. "Thanks for all your help," he said to Lily before looking at Molly. "And thank you for having me. Say goodbye to Grant for me, would you?" Blake started moving toward the door.

"Of course," Molly said. She hurried ahead of him and opened the door. "Bye. Take care of that little girl."

"I will." Feeling the weight of responsibility bearing down on him, he went outside, down the cement stairs and headed to his car. He swung the carrier and Peyton's crying went down a notch. Maybe she'd follow tradition and fall asleep in the car. But then she might not sleep tonight, and that meant he wouldn't sleep, and tomorrow would be a bigger challenge than usual. The cycle went on and on.

Now he knew why God intended for kids to have two parents—to split the duties. What he would give for someone to help him out. But he was alone as a parent, with no one else to depend on. Though many people managed in his plight, he wasn't sure he could do this by himself.

All of a sudden his stomach hollowed out and a feeling of hopelessness washed over him. He put the baby carrier down and leaned a hand on the window of the car and bowed his head for a moment.

Lord, how in the world am I going to cope with everything? Please, give me the strength to do so.

"Blake!"

He straightened and turned. Lily was heading out the door toward his car. Just the sight of her eased something inside of him, made him feel somehow less alone. Odd, since he barely knew her. He frowned slightly. He must be punchy from lack of sleep.

He unlocked the car and waited for her.

"You forgot your coat." She held it out.

"Oh, thanks." He took the coat from her. "Well, tonight was a bust." He lifted the baby seat into the car.

"Not entirely." Lily leaned in and stroked Peyton's cheek. "I got to see this little lady."

"And me," he joked. Oh, man, where had that come from?

Lily pulled her chin in, blinking. "Um… yeah, that, too."

"Ignore me," he said, shaking his head in bemusement. "I was just teasing."

"I know," she said, shoving her hands in her pants pockets. "And…it was good to see you."

"It was?"

"Well, sure. You need to get out."

Oh, that was what she meant. "Yeah, but I don't see that happening much for a while. I've got my hands pretty full."

"I know. Let me know if I can help."

He nodded. Hopefully it wouldn't come to that. He was probably worrying for nothing.

"Okay, then." Lily turned to the house.

Peyton let out a squawk and then started wailing again.

Lily spun back around. "Try not to worry too much," she said. "Kids get sick and they get better."

"I'll try," he said, closing the car door.

"And in case you didn't know, The Market Pantry on the far south end of Main Street is open late."

"Thank you," he said.

She waved and then went up the stairs and disappeared inside.

Blake got in the car, and then started it. As soon as the engine turned over, Peyton's crying ramped up. He gripped the steering wheel, feeling overwhelmed, drained and more alone than ever.

A break. He needed a break. And maybe a fill-in babysitter. Again, Lily came to mind. Was she the answer to his prayers?

With that question hovering in his mind and exhaustion hovering at the edges of his brain, he pulled out into the street and headed in the direction of The Market Pantry to get Peyton's medicine.

It was going to be another sleepless night in a long line of many.

Lily hurried back into the house, and as soon as the door closed behind her, Molly stepped into the living room.

"You get him all situated?" she asked, her eyebrows lifted slightly.

"He forgot his coat," Lily said breezily.

"You seemed awfully anxious to say another goodbye to him." Molly smirked. "Grant said you almost ripped the coat out of his hands to take it out yourself."

Maybe Lily had been a little grabby, though she'd tried not to be. But she wasn't admitting it to Molly. Molly would latch on to that tidbit and take it to a place Lily wasn't going. "There was no ripping involved."

"He's very handsome," Molly said, coming at Lily from another angle. She was clearly fishing.

"You think?" Lily asked, looking as if she hadn't considered Blake's gorgeousness at all.

"What? You don't find him attractive?"

Lily paused. "I didn't say that," Lily said, stopping short of lying.

"So you *do* find him attractive!" Molly said triumphantly.

"No harm in that," Lily said, rationalizing both to herself and Molly. "Don't get your hopes up." Molly had met and married Grant over a year ago, and since she'd found true love, she wanted the same for Lily. Desperately. And while Lily was happy for Molly, happy-ever-after wasn't on Lily's radar right now. Winning *Project Fashion* was.

"But you *did* notice him."

"I'd have to be dead not to notice him." Lily was nothing if not pragmatic.

"Okay. You've *really* noticed him." Molly cast Lily a brightly inquisitive look. "So...what did you think?"

Lily sighed. Molly wasn't going to let up. And truth be told, Lily could use a shoulder. Maybe she should just spill and move on. "Well, I've actually been thinking about him a lot since we met." As in all night long.

Molly moved in closer. "Really?"

"Yeah, and I have to say, it has me worried." Lily nibbled on her bottom lip.

"You're not interested in a romance," Molly said. She and Lily had talked at length about Lily's goals, and her desire not to be tied down with any kind of commitment so she would be free to go after *Project Fashion*. "And I get it." Molly sank down onto the couch. "I didn't want to fall for Grant, either. But sometimes we don't have a choice in matters of the heart."

"I choose and my heart listens," Lily replied, lifting her chin. Or, that was the goal, at least. Think it, live it. Right.

"So why are you worried?" Trust Molly not to pull any punches. "Just move on with your plans and don't give Blake a second thought."

Lily opened her mouth to give Molly a retort, but quickly closed it. Lily stayed silent for a moment, then decided she needed to unload more or she'd go crazy. "Something about him draws me in."

"Aha. Now we're getting somewhere."

Yes, maybe they were getting somewhere. Lily warmed to the subject. Maybe hashing it out would bring some clarity to the situation. And help her grow some semblance of a backbone. "Sure, he's gorgeous."

"Very."

"But there's also something else about him. A...vulnerability, maybe, that really calls to me." Whatever it was, she was having a hard time pinning it down. She gnashed her teeth.

"Well, he has been through a lot lately."

"I know. And he's got this delightful baby to take care of, and he's completely clueless about that, and he has this business to run." Lily shook her head. "I don't know, I just find myself thinking about him a lot and I don't want to be distracted by him."

"You don't want any roadblocks."

"Right. I'm on the cusp of moving forward with something I've waited a long time for. I can't just set all that aside, you know." Lily sat down next to Molly. "I'm too close to get sidetracked now." A thought occurred to Lily. "But...being attracted to someone isn't the be-all and end-all." She warmed to her thoughts. "In fact, people are attracted to other people all the time, and it means nothing, goes nowhere, right?"

Molly looked at Lily sideways. "Um...yes..."

"So rather than deny the truth, I'm just going to accept it, voice it and that will be that." Lily straightened her shoulders. "I'm attracted to Blake Stonely and I'm not going to let it bother me. I'm just going to get on with my life, business as usual." She waited, half expecting a lightning bolt to strike her down from above.

But nothing happened. She sighed inwardly as relief spread through her.

"Feel better?" Molly asked.

"Yes, actually, I do. I've acknowledged my attraction to Blake out loud." Lily stood. "Now I can forget about him."

"You think it will be that easy?" Molly asked, her voice coated in skepticism. "I thought I could just ignore my feelings for Grant, too, and we both know how that turned out."

With an engagement. And then a wedding. Their very own happy ending.

Lily scrambled for a foothold to support her argument. "It'll be fine. I don't have any reason to see Blake again. I'll just putter along in my lane and soon enough I'll be on my way to LA to win *Project Fashion*." And her heart would stay just how she chose.

"So you think out of sight, out of mind?"

"Exactly."

Molly gave her a look rife with doubt. "Let me know how that works for you."

Lily shrugged off Molly's disbelief. "It'll be fine. I'm busy, or will be when I get a job, and he's busy, too. Pretty soon he'll be nothing but a memory in my rearview mirror."

She was back on track. *Yes*. She felt better. Strong. Safe. Resolute. Perfect!

Free from worry about her fascination with Blake, she changed the subject. "Hey, do you still want me to help you plan the Valentine's Day dance?" The singles' group held a dance every year in honor of the most romantic day of the year. Lily went for the dancing, her second most favorite thing after designing clothes.

"Yes, definitely," Molly said. "I was thinking of an '80s theme this year."

"Oooh, great idea. Nothing like a good hairband song to get this girl on the floor."

Molly grinned. "I thought you'd like that."

An idea occurred to Lily. "I can go through my dad's album collection for the music."

"And I'll have Grant transfer the tunes into digital format."

"He won't mind?"

"He's a techno geek. He'll love it." Grant, a former programmer, owned a computer repair/ software development company, which he ran from a Main Street storefront right next door to Molly's store, Bow Wow Boutique, a designer pet store.

"Good point," Lily said. "I'll go through the albums soon, and then get them to him in the next week or so." Valentine's Day was still a few weeks away.

"I'll let him know," Molly said. "We should also make a trip to Party Depot in Pacific City for supplies." Moonlight Cove lacked any kind of party supply store.

"Just let me know when you want to go," Lily said.

"Will do."

They rejoined the group in the family room and Lily relaxed and enjoyed the activities Grant and Molly had planned, as well as the cookies-and-cream cupcakes Grant's aunt Rose Kincaid had baked for the event. Lily realized how much she'd needed a bit of socializing after the stress of her fruitless job search, and she was glad she'd decided to attend the event.

An hour after her conversation with Molly, Lily said her goodbyes, left and headed home, brainstorming job possibilities as she navigated the rain-slicked streets to the other side of town. She'd heard that a restaurant in the next town up the coast was hiring, and that perhaps the local dentist needed a receptionist while the regular gal went on maternity leave. Two leads to follow up on in the morning. One way or another, she had to find a job as soon as possible.

Just as she pulled into the driveway, her

cell phone trilled. She pulled it from her coat pocket and checked the caller ID.

Blake Stonely. Lily's heart did a little blip. Why was he calling? Her finger hovered over Answer, but she didn't press it. She needed to gather herself before she talked to him. She didn't know why, exactly. She was feeling her way here, and right now, she needed to deal with Blake via voice mail rather than by talking directly to him. Call her weak.

Eventually the ringing stopped. After about thirty seconds, a different sound came from her phone signaling she had a voice mail. With a quivery touch she punched the buttons to listen to the message, then held the phone up to her ear.

"Hey, Lily, it's Blake Stonely." A pause. *"Listen, I hate to impose, but my sitter called and she has a bad case of pneumonia and she's going to be out indefinitely."* A sigh came through. *"Worse yet, Peyton is still running a fever, so I can't take her to the store tomorrow. I hate to do this, but I was wondering if I could take you up on your offer to help out for a while, until my sitter is back on her feet. I'd pay you, of course."* He cleared his throat. *"So, um, call me as soon as you can. Thanks."*

Lily clicked End Call and stared out the front window, her phone clutched in her hand. What was she going to do? Helping Blake wouldn't exactly be out of sight, out of mind. In fact, coming to his rescue was the exact opposite of what she'd mapped out.

She let out a shaky breath, feeling torn. He was in a bind. She needed the money, and working for him for a bit would ease the job hunting pressure for a while. Would it really be smart to refuse a paying job?

Probably not.

Lily tapped a finger on her knee. Helping Blake was the right thing to do all around. She couldn't turn him down. She didn't have the heart to say no when he desperately needed her help, even though doing so felt like a distinct threat to her at the moment.

Bubbles of anxiety churned around inside of her like a rough ocean, setting her nerves on a jagged edge. She'd definitely have to find a way to work for Blake while keeping him at a safe distance.

She'd worked too hard, dreamed of being on *Project Fashion* for too long, to let anything derail her dreams now.

Chapter Three

Lily pulled into Blake's driveway, her gaze roaming over the cute little 1940s house on Fogcutter Street, just east of downtown. His single-story home featured white paint, dark blue shutters flanking the windows and a wide front porch that was bare at the moment but would be a perfect place for a glider or swing.

The large lot had plenty of grass, lovely southern exposure and a picket fence running across the front yard. An ugly gray one that leaned to one side and had a few slats missing, but a picket fence nonetheless. The yard was a bit overgrown and neglected looking right now; clearly Blake didn't have much time for gardening.

Little wonder, with everything he had going on.

Even so, it was a perfect house, replete with

just the right amount of charm and old-fashioned flavor she loved so much.

Not that she'd ever live here. But the designer in her could see the potential and she could admire from afar.

She parked next to his compact car and sat for a moment, getting her nerves under control. She reiterated that she'd done the right thing by agreeing to babysit Peyton, both for Blake and for herself. She had to quit letting the prospect of working for him get to her. She was determined to contain her attraction and focus on Peyton. She could do this while remaining detached.

Taking a revitalizing breath, she climbed out of her car and hurried to the door, dodging raindrops. Even before she stood in front of the red wooden door, she could hear Peyton crying inside. Oh, boy. Blake had clearly been having a rough time.

She raised her hand to knock, but before she could, the door swung open.

A harried-looking Blake stood there with a screaming Peyton hoisted up over one shoulder. His hair was mussed and he had dark circles under his eyes. His jeans and T-shirt looked as if he'd slept—or perhaps not?—in them. He'd been through the wringer.

But he was still gorgeous. Of course. Maybe

she'd been wishing he'd turn unattractive over-night? Not happening. Ever. She had to deal with it.

"Hey," he said with a definitely weary edge to his voice. "Come on in."

Lily stepped inside, determined to focus on the practical aspects of the situation. She made quick note of the living room, which was comprised of a tan microfiber love seat and sofa, dark wooden accent furniture and a large big-screen TV set at an angle in one corner. Nice, but bland. Very clean. But perfectly imper-sonal.

And...wow, there were vacuum marks in the carpet, as if he'd just vacuumed one minute ago. How odd. In her book, vacuuming would fall to just about last on the list if she were tak-ing care of a fussy baby solo.

She turned her attention to Peyton. "She sounds like she doesn't feel very well."

"No, she doesn't." As he spoke, he shifted Peyton so she was lying down in his arms. Without missing a beat, he started the swing, swing, swing technique Lily had shown him a couple of days ago.

"Look at you," she said, putting her purse on the couch that sat just to the left of the front door. "You're a pro."

He gave her a tired look edged in desperation. "Not really. I swung her like this all night long, and she still didn't sleep much." He yawned. "And neither did I."

Lily held her hands up. "You want me to try?"

"Definitely," he said, coming closer. "Here you go."

He bent down slightly so the baby was at Lily's level, and a whiff of his woodsy, masculine-smelling aftershave wafted through the air, right to her nose. It was all she could do to hold out her hands steadily as he transferred Peyton to her.

His arms touched Lily's and she felt her knees tremble and her tummy somersaulted. She steeled herself and took the baby, keeping her in a prone position, trying to ignore Blake, which was about as easy as trying to ignore breathing.

"I've got her," Lily managed, but her voice came out breathily. She zeroed in on Peyton's red face, and then as soon as was practically possible Lily scooted away into the safety zone.

Able to breathe again, Lily started the swing, concentrating on Peyton rather than her wonderful-smelling uncle. She walked over to the big picture window that looked out over the front yard and did her baby calming there, moving in a small circle.

Hold the baby close. Swing, swing, swing. Ignore the attractive man across the room. Rinse. Repeat.

After a few circles, Peyton's cries quieted. Lily kept it up and added a little extra flare at the end of each swing to further soothe Peyton. Her brother Liam always liked that motion.

From the corner of her eye, Lily saw Blake watching her intently, his hands on his hips. She tried to ignore him, but that proved impossible. Suddenly self-conscious, she went against her instincts and met his gaze.

His blue eyes grabbed on to her gaze.

"What are you doing?" she said in a loud whisper.

"I'm watching."

She froze and a tingle ran up her spine. "Watching?"

"Your technique," he said quietly. "Clearly you have some kind of magic way of soothing her. I'm watching and learning."

"Oh. Of course." She swallowed. So he was *learning*. It still unnerved her to have his gaze glued to her. "You'll get the hang of it."

He ran a hand over his face. "I hope so. This no-sleeping thing is going to catch up with me any day now." Blinking, he shook his head. "Maybe it already has."

"Good thing you have an unlimited supply of caffeine waiting for you at work," Lily said, looking for levity. Anything to counterbalance the off-balance way his scrutiny made her feel.

He smiled. "Yeah, I never thought of that."

"Well, there you go." She looked down at Peyton. "She's almost asleep. Where do you want her?"

He crooked a thumb over his shoulder. "Follow me."

He headed down the hall to the right and Lily followed, keeping her steps fluid and smooth in the interest of keeping Peyton asleep. They passed two bedrooms and then, at the end of the hall, he went into the third one.

Lily stepped into the room. Gray morning light spilled in from the large window on the wall directly across from the door. The walls were plain white and devoid of any decorations. An oak crib with pink bumpers sat against one wall and there was a changing table nearby and a matching dresser, too, upon which sat a baby monitor. A bentwood rocker graced the near corner of the room. Two baskets of neatly folded laundry sat in front of the closet.

Blake went to the crib and pulled the fuzzy pink blankets back, looking Lily's way. She got the message and moved in and gingerly lifted Peyton into the crib and laid her down on her back. As Lily withdrew her arms, she held her breath in hopes the baby would sleep on even though she wasn't held snugly in Lily's arms.

After a moment, Peyton let out a little whimper, stiffening and flailing a little hand in the air. Lily froze and she saw Blake do the same. But then the baby settled, and finally she slept, her little bow mouth working as she drifted off.

Lily looked at Blake, nodding. She mouthed, "She's asleep."

He nodded, then pointed to the door.

Lily turned and tiptoed out.

Blake followed, pulling the door closed behind him but leaving it ajar, pointing down the hall, indicating Lily should go back into the living room.

She headed to the other end of the house, mentally ticking off a checklist that had been forming in her head ever since she'd agreed to be Peyton's nanny. Get fussy baby to sleep—check. Now, if she could simply meet and defeat the challenge of keeping her interest in Blake strictly professional, she'd be cool.

When she reached the living room, she turned, intending to ask Blake about Peyton's meal schedule.

Before she could speak, Blake bowed with

a flourish. "I bow down to you, oh wise and wonderful baby whisperer." He straightened. "Please, share your secrets with me, the lowly man who's deprived of sleep."

She smiled, liking this playful side of him. Unable to resist his bantering, she held her hand up, palm out. "Please, please. Save your applause for later."

He cocked his head at an angle. "Oh, so you think I'm joking?"

She blinked. "Aren't you?"

"Not even close," he said. "I thought it was a fluke when you managed to get her to sleep at The Cabana the other day. But now?" He shook his head. "You seem to have some kind of charmed way of getting Miss Fussypants to sleep."

She raised an eyebrow. "Are you stressed out?"

He frowned.

"Just bear with me," she said. "Are you stressed out?"

"Yeah, I am," he said, rolling his shoulders. "I've got a business to run and a sick baby to take care of."

"So you're understandably tense. I get it. You have every right to be that way." She smoothed a stray lock of hair behind her ear. "The thing is, babies can sense tension, and from my experience with my brothers and sisters, they tend to feed on it."

"So I'm passing my tenseness on to Peyton?"

"To some extent, yes."

His face fell.

"Not on purpose, of course," she quickly said. "But my point is this. If you relax, she'll relax."

"I don't even know what relaxing is these days," he said with a grimace. "I just run from one crisis to another."

His life sounded insanely chaotic. No wonder he and Peyton weren't getting any rest. He was overwhelmed.

He looked at his watch, punctuating her thoughts about how busy he was. "Oh, wow, it's getting late. Why don't we go into the kitchen and I'll go over things."

"Good idea."

He turned and headed through a doorway that, presumably, led to the kitchen.

Lily followed, curious to see the rest of the house.

She stepped into the kitchen and drew up short, taken aback at the room's obvious lack of personality. The counters were devoid of anything, and the stainless steel appliances sparkled with nary a fingerprint visible. The tile floor sparkled, and a vague hint of floor cleaner hung in the air.

Had he actually mopped the floor this morning? And vacuumed, too?

She shifted her gaze around. The small breakfast nook held a small round table that had the chairs arranged around it in perfect precision, as if they'd been placed using a ruler. And the window above the gleaming stainless steel sink was so clear she would have sworn there was no glass in its panes.

It was a spare, cleaned-to-within-an-inch-of-its-life space and held no personal touches or evidence that anyone had ever eaten—much less cooked or enjoyed—a meal within the walls of the room.

In fact, the whole house smacked of a blank, antiseptic cleanliness that set her back a bit. She'd grown up in a messy, relaxed household, one where cleaning only happened when absolutely necessary. This place was so impersonal, so cold it made her sad.

She slanted her gaze to Blake. He opened a drawer and pulled out a pad of paper and a pen.

She swallowed a comment about the odd sterility of the place out of politeness. But the room spoke volumes about Blake and what was important to him.

And she had a sneaking suspicion she'd just agreed to work for a control freak of major proportions.

At about 11:00 a.m., during a lull in business—okay, the whole morning had been one big lull—Blake left the front counter in Jonah's care and headed into his office to catch up on paperwork.

He was going to run an ad in the *Moonlight Cove Gazette* offering a two-for-one coffee deal on Tuesdays from noon to five as a way to drum up business. He couldn't afford a graphic designer, so he was going to come up with something himself. He sat down behind his desk and booted up his computer, then went to the file he'd saved that contained the rough idea he'd come up with using a template he'd found on the internet. He put on his artist hat and tried to come up with something that was simple yet eye-catching.

His mind turned to Peyton. Poor little thing. Though her temperature had been normal when he'd left home, he still worried. He'd done a bit of research on the internet this morning and had read that viruses in infants her age could quickly turn serious.

Maybe he should check in with Lily again.

Yeah, he would. He wouldn't be able to focus on his work until he did. He dug his cell phone out of his pocket and swiped it on. Then he went to Contacts and pressed the button for Lily he'd created while he'd been going over instructions with her this morning.

He tapped his fingers on his desk while the phone rang on the other end. After five rings, Lily answered. "Hello?" No crying in the background. That was good.

"Hi, it's me," he said, his shoulders tensing.

"I know it's you."

Right. Her phone would tell her that. He got to the heart of the matter. "How's Peyton?"

"She's the same as she was when you called an hour ago."

Had it only been an hour? "Still sleeping?"

"No, she's awake now, and I'm making lunch."

"Any fever?" he asked, praying it was still down.

"No, she feels cool to the touch."

Some of the tension in his shoulders eased. "Did you need to change her diaper?"

A sigh echoed through the line. "Yes, I did need to, and I did."

He stood up. "The diaper disposer is in her closet—"

"I know, you showed me where it was."

"Oh, yeah." He rose and paused, the outside of his thigh propped against his desk. "What's for lunch?"

A moment of silence. "Blake, do you trust me?"

"Yes," he said immediately. "Of course." Lily was levelheaded and smart, and had lots of experience with babies.

"Then you need to quit calling every hour and let me take care of Peyton."

He grimaced. "I'm bothering you, aren't I?"

"You're concerned, I get that. But what's the point of having me here if you're doing all the work remotely?"

"I hadn't thought of that." She made a good point.

"I have this handled. I've got nothing else to do but focus on Peyton. Let me do that, and I promise if anything changes or if I have a question, I'll call."

He rubbed the bridge of his nose. "I'm over-controlling."

"A bit, yes. But with the best of intentions," she said softly.

"I'm glad you see it that way." Some people wouldn't be so gracious; his need for control wasn't always received well. Amy had chided him for the trait endlessly.

"Definitely. But you have to allow yourself

some distance so you can take care of The Cabana. That's why you hired me, right?"

"Right."

"Then let me do my job, and I'll be in touch if I need anything."

"Okay." He needed to back off.

"Would it make you feel better if I checked in every few hours?"

"Yes, probably."

"Then that's what I'll do." She paused. "Let's see. It's just after eleven. How about I check in at two?"

"Um, well…" He chewed on the inside of his cheek. "That seems like a long time."

"Okay, how about one-thirty?"

"Sounds good." Surely he could go two and a half hours without checking in.

"I'll talk to you then." A moment passed. "Oh, and, Blake?"

"Yes?"

"Don't worry. I've got this covered."

His tense shoulders eased down all the way. "I know you do," he said truthfully. "You're very capable. Peyton's in excellent hands, I know that." Lily was better with Peyton than he was.

"Okay, then. Try to relax. Bye."

"Bye."

He pressed End and shoved his cell into his

pants pocket. Boy, did he feel foolish. He'd been a pest this morning. In his defense, though, this was the first time he'd left an ill Peyton. He'd never imagined how hard it would be to turn over her care to someone else when she wasn't feeling well. All of his protective instincts were on high alert.

He sat back down behind his desk. He had to find a way to let go of Peyton during the workday or The Cabana would be toast. He trusted Lily implicitly. She'd really saved the day by agreeing to fill in for Mrs. Jones. And the last thing he wanted was for her to think he didn't have faith in her. He had to quit bugging her and rest assured that she would call if Peyton took a turn for the worse.

A turn for the worse. A chill of dread skated up his spine. Peyton was so little, so young and vulnerable. He had to protect Peyton and keep her safe. It killed him not to be with her right now.

He looked at his computer screen and frowned. The ad was a mess. He was no graphic artist; in fact, he didn't have an artistic bone in his body. Looked as if he had his work cut out for him at work. Nothing new there. Although only recently had he had to deal with business problems while also trying to take care of an infant.

Once again, the challenge of being a single dad with a foundering business to run hit him square in the gut, creating a sickening tension that never seemed to go away.

He was in over his head.

How in the world was he going to make his life work right now without neglecting Peyton or The Cabana? Was that lofty goal even possible? He looked at the ad on his computer screen and thought of a sick little baby at home whom he couldn't even take care of himself.

A prayer rose to mind: *Lord, I need Your help right now, more than ever.*

Because Blake sincerely believed anything short of complete disaster would be a blessing.

Chapter Four

Crooning to the baby in her arms, Lily walked the circuit around the inside of Blake's house as she tried to get Peyton back to sleep after being awake since lunch.

Fortunately Peyton had taken a two-hour nap this morning, and Lily had been able to get some sketching done for the new line of teen clothes she was designing. Although she had no prospects to sell the line to, she took time to practice her craft as often as possible.

But now, in the late afternoon, poor Peyton was fussy. Her fever had spiked back up an hour ago and her nose had started to run. Obviously she didn't feel well, and she just didn't want to settle down. Hopefully the infant fever reducer Lily had given her would kick in soon and Peyton would drift off and sleep a bit. Not that Lily minded her being awake. Not at all.

But for Peyton's sake, some rest was necessary to fight the virus.

Plus, Lily really wanted to be able to tell Blake she'd been able to get Lily to sleep. From his numerous phone calls it was obvious he was stressed out about leaving Peyton while she was ill, and he clearly trusted Lily to take care of his niece. He'd been ready to close the store down to come home when she'd called him an hour ago and reported that Peyton's fever was back and that she had a runny nose.

Lily had talked him out of that idea, convincing him she had it handled. She would consider it a failure if she couldn't report that Peyton had gotten plenty of rest and had had a reasonably calm day when Blake did come home after dinner. Lily took her baby care responsibilities very seriously.

There was more, though, she thought as she stopped in the kitchen to take a sip of water from her glass on the counter. Though she would die before she admitted it out loud, she had an insane desire to impress Blake by going above and beyond being a competent babysitter who did a good job. She wanted him to be in awe of her. Total awe.

She put down her glass and, while still rocking a whimpering Peyton, looked out the window above the sink, watching the rain come down, reiterating the parameters she'd laid out for herself regarding Blake. She was going for a neutral, employee/employer relationship with him, not the I-must-impress-this-man nonsense that seemed to be gripping her. She had to stop wanting to astonish and amaze Blake. As long as he thought she was a decent babysitter that was enough.

She felt Peyton relax and looked down at the baby. Ah. Finally asleep. Lily turned from the window and started to head to Peyton's room to put her down in her crib, hoping the baby wouldn't wake up during the transfer. But just as she reached the middle of the kitchen she heard a sound coming from the living room. Her heart skittered. She froze and cocked her head, listening intently. There. A rattle… or maybe a scrape! Her breathing hitched. It sounded as if someone were trying to get into the house!

She went into baby-protection mode. Her gaze flew around and landed on Peyton's bouncy seat sitting on the floor by the kitchen table. Soundlessly Lily went over and ever-so-carefully put the sleeping infant into the seat and secured her with the Y strap. Peyton slept on as Lily slid the bouncy seat over so it was hidden behind the table.

Whirling as she stood, Lily frantically searched for a weapon. Nothing on the counters. She remembered seeing a knife drawer when she'd made lunch, so she stealthily went over, slid the drawer open and grabbed the largest knife she could see. Armed, she tiptoed across the kitchen and took her stand next to the island.

The distinct sound of footsteps carried to her. Someone was in the house!

Her fingers gripped the knife handle. "Whoever you are, I have a knife," she shouted, holding the blade out in front of her, ready to strike. "Don't come any closer." Her heart thundered in her chest, and all she could think of was that she had to keep Peyton safe…

For a moment, the footsteps stopped and silence reigned. Then someone called out, "Lily, don't stab me! It's Blake."

Lily dropped the hand holding the knife to her side. *What?* "Blake?" she called incredulously.

He stepped into the kitchen, his hands held high. "See, it's just me," he said sheepishly.

Her free hand pressed to her chest. "You scared the living daylights out of me!" She set the knife on the island with a clatter. "What are you doing home?" He'd very succinctly told her he'd be closing tonight and that he wouldn't be home until after eight.

"I was worried about Peyton, so I trained Jonah to close and he stayed."

His concern for Peyton made her feel all mushy inside, which Lily tried to ignore. Instead, she glared at him. "Did it occur to you to call and let me in on your plan so I'd be prepared for you to come through the door instead of thinking someone was breaking in?"

He shrugged. "Yes, but I didn't want the phone to wake up Peyton if she was sleeping." His gaze skittered around. "Where is she?"

Lily went over and pointed to the hidden bouncy seat. "I hid her over here," she said, lowering her voice.

Blake smiled and came all the way into the kitchen. His eyes touched on the knife abandoned on the island. "Would you really have used that knife?" he whispered.

"You bet I would have," she said in quiet voice, raising her chin. "I thought a stranger was breaking in. I wasn't going to just let someone saunter in and get to Peyton, or me, without putting up a fight."

"You were protecting Peyton," he stated, his gaze going soft.

"Of course I was." She picked up the knife and went over to put it away. "Isn't that my job?"

"Well, yes. But a lot of people would have just cowered in the corner."

"Well, I guess I'm not a lot of people," she said. "I take my responsibilities very seriously."

"I see that," he said solemnly, taking off his rain-splashed coat. "Can you forgive me for taking a few years off your life?"

"I'll think about it," she said dramatically, which clearly indicated he was being silly for asking.

"Whew." He lifted one side of his mouth into a crooked grin. "You had me worried."

She liked that he "got" her snark.

As he laid his coat over the back of one of the chairs, he craned his neck to look at Peyton. "She's out."

"Yep," Lily said, doing her best not to notice how wavy the rain had made his hair. "She needs the rest."

"You think her fever's down?" he asked, his brow creased.

"She felt cooler when she went to sleep."

"The medication kicked in." He frowned. "Shouldn't she be better already?"

She held a finger to her mouth and pointed to the hallway.

He got the message and headed to the living room.

Once there, she said, "It's only been a few days, and viruses can hang around for a long time." Larry and Liam, who always got sick at the same time—they shared everything, including germs—had perpetual colds when they were little. They were, literally, the snottiest kids on the block.

"And now she has a runny nose." Blake looked down, then back up at Lily. "That means she's worse, right?"

Possibly. But Lily didn't want to feed his concern. So she said, "Don't worry. She'll be fine once the germ runs its course."

"I don't like seeing her sick," he said, his voice husky. "I couldn't get her off my mind all day."

"So you came home early." Honestly, his leaving work for Peyton really touched her. A lot of people wouldn't have come home for an ill kid. And many people, like her mom, simply couldn't without losing valuable income. Luckily, Mom had Lily to fill in. Blake didn't have a built-in support system. He was on his own, and was clearly struggling with the dual responsibilities of his job and caring for Peyton.

"Yeah." He shrugged. "I know, lame."

She thought it was wonderful. "It's not lame at all. It just means you care about her."

"In Anna's stead I have to take care of her, no matter what."

His dedication lit up a warm spot inside of her. "You are," Lily said, resisting the urge to touch him, offer comfort. She had to keep in mind the limits she'd set up.

"It's hard not being here," he told her. "I feel like I'm abandoning her."

Lily drew her eyebrows together. "Why would you think that? You've left her well cared for," she replied firmly.

"I didn't mean to imply that you're somehow lacking as a caretaker," he said.

"I didn't think that."

"I just think a parent should be there for their kids." A shadow formed in his eyes, turning them a darker shade of blue.

Lily looked at him closely, noting the tenseness in his shoulders and the firmness of his lips. His statement, and body language, spoke volumes, though she wasn't sure what they were saying. Only that somehow, someway, he had personal experience to back up his opinion.

Oh, how she'd love to know more about him. But she wasn't comfortable prying, and getting to know Blake on a deeper level wouldn't exactly be keeping their relationship impersonal. The exact opposite, in fact. So she squashed the questions on her tongue and said, "You can rely on others for help. All parents do. My mom left my siblings with me all the time."

Too much, actually. Though she loved her mom and siblings, she'd always resented being relied upon so much. That was why she was so anxious to finally be able to follow her dream and get on *Project Fashion*. After years of being tied down by caring for her brothers and sisters, now was her time. She had a feeling if she didn't leave Moonlight Cove now, she never would. She had to break free.

"I'd rather rely on myself when I can," Blake said succinctly as he moved over and pulled the curtains closed on the picture window that looked out over the front yard and street. "Life is easier when I know what to expect."

She sensed a world of information behind his statement; she just couldn't decipher what it all meant.

Before she could reply, his cell phone rang and he held up a hand as he pulled the device out of his pocket and looked at it. "It's Jonah," he said. "I need to take this."

She nodded. "Go ahead."

He turned and went out of the room as he pressed the cell to his ear. "Hey, Jonah. What's up?"

Lily watched him go, her curiosity about him at an all-time high. He'd confirmed what she'd already figured out—he wanted control in all facets of his life. He also had strong beliefs about the parent/child relationship. What had caused all that? Why did he want to keep things so well-ordered, so perfectly perfect?

She had a feeling he had an interesting story to tell. And, oh, boy, would she like to know all about it—

With swift precision she cut that thought off. She could not—*would* not—let herself wonder about what had made Blake the way he was. Didn't matter. Just as it didn't matter that she appreciated how he'd come home early because he was worried about Peyton. Or that she was moved by how he was determined to protect his niece.

All that mattered was that this job was temporary, and as soon as it was over, Lily would be moving on with her plans to get herself on *Project Fashion*. She wasn't letting herself get sidetracked.

Not even for an enigmatic man who seemed to become more interesting—and compelling—every time she saw him.

* * *

His heart hanging so low it felt as if it were in his feet, Blake hung up from his call with Jonah. Figured that the one time he left someone else in charge, something went wrong.

He went in search of Lily and found her sitting at the kitchen table, a large sketchbook open on the table in front of her.

"Watcha doing?" he asked.

"Working on my designs."

He craned his neck. "Can I see?"

"Sure." She spun the sketchbook around.

The page was filled with a myriad of pencil sketches of what were clearly summery clothes that to his untrained eye seemed designed to appeal to younger women. Teens, maybe? "Wow. Those look good."

She smiled. "Thanks. I'm starting to design a collection of summer wear for teens. I always start out with what I call stream of consciousness drawing."

"What's that?"

"I just draw whatever comes to me, as quickly as possible. Then I winnow down the drawings, look for common design themes and start building the line on those core elements."

Impressive. "Looks like you have the process down."

"I like to think so, but I'll always have more to learn."

"Did you go to design school?"

A shadow passed over her face. "No. I was accepted into a school in Portland when I graduated from high school, but my mom needed me here."

"Oh, wow. That's rough." She'd sacrificed a lot for her family.

"Yeah, I was disappointed."

"I'll bet. But now it looks like you're on the right track. Molly told me about your plans for LA."

"I hope so. I've honed my skills over the years and read everything I could get my hands on about clothing design. It's time for me to make the leap."

"I'm sure you'll do great." She struck him as the kind of person who accomplished everything she put her mind to.

"I've waited a long time to be able to do my own thing. I don't want to have to come back a failure."

He knew what that was like, not that he'd tell her about his own crash and burn in New York. "I sincerely doubt you'll fail. Hey, listen, Jonah used the wrong soap and overflowed the dishwasher at the store, and I have to go help him fix it."

"Oh, wow. Sounds like a mess."

"Yeah, he said there's a lot of water and suds on the floor." Wonderful. Just the way Blake wanted to spend his evening. "Do you think you could stay here with Peyton for a while longer?" If she said no, he'd have to take Peyton with him, and that just didn't seem like a good idea.

"Sure," Lily said. "In fact, I saw some frozen hamburger in the freezer. Would you like me to defrost it and make something for dinner?"

Her offer took him by surprise, but then again, not so much. Lily was clearly a giver. He shook his head. "As tempting as it is to say yes to a homemade meal, I don't expect you to cook."

"I'm not talking anything gourmet. I was thinking something along the lines of hamburger beef Stroganoff made with the condensed soup I saw in the pantry."

"Actually, that sounds delicious." He wasn't much of a cook and got by on frozen dinners and deli food purchased at the local grocery store.

"It's an old standby in our house."

"Well, I appreciate the offer, but I don't feel right agreeing."

"You sure? Peyton's asleep, and I have my designs to work on. I'm happy to stay."

He pondered that. It would be well after the dinner hour when he returned, and he'd undoubtedly be starving…

"And if I make dinner, you get more time with Peyton," Lily added, a gleam in her eyes.

True. And he was anxious to have some quality time with the baby after being gone all day. "In that case, all right. But this is a one-time thing. Cooking is not in your job description."

"Agreed," she said, holding a hand over her heart. "I'll go get the hamburger out now," she said, brushing by him, her arm touching his on the way. "I think I saw some salad in the fridge, too."

"Lily?" he said, doing his best to disregard how his skin tingled where she'd touched him.

She swung around, her green eyes questioning. "Yes?"

"Thank you," he said softly. "Once again, you've saved my bacon." It seemed to be what she did best.

"You're welcome." Her face lit up. "Ooooh, bacon," she said. "I saw some of that in the fridge. Maybe we'll have hamburgers with bacon instead." With a bounce in her step she headed off in the direction of the kitchen, a bundle of energy he couldn't seem to ignore.

He let out a big breath and refocused his

attention on the latest crisis at hand—Jonah and the exploding dishwasher. He didn't have the time—or inclination—to be preoccupied with Lily. He had enough on his plate already. Too much, actually. He'd be a complete fool to add a romance into the mix. Besides, he wanted to be in complete control of his own heart.

He went into the kitchen to take a last look at Peyton, who was still sleeping like a rock in her bouncy seat. He laid the barest touch on her head, loving the feel of her downy hair beneath his fingers. He hated to leave her again, and he felt pulled in two different directions, as if he were being torn in half.

Would he ever be whole again? Right now, it seemed as if the answer to that question was a resounding and distressing *no*.

The moment Blake stepped back into his house, he took off his figurative plumber's hat and put on his daddy fedora. With an anxiousness that surprised him, he went into the kitchen to see Peyton. His mouth watered when he detected the smell of cooking hamburger. He was starving.

Lily met him in the hall with Peyton in her arms. A *sleeping* Peyton. "She just fell back asleep," Lily said in a whisper. "I was on my way to put her to bed."

Disappointment grabbed him and shook hard; he'd really been looking forward to holding Peyton. "Okay." He wasn't about to wake a sleeping baby. "Let me kiss her good-night."

Lily paused, then turned a bit so Peyton was toward him. "Okay."

Bending down, he pressed a kiss to Peyton's forehead, trying to pay no attention to how close he was to Lily. Instead he focused on the softness of Peyton's fuzz-topped head and inhaling the wonderful scent of baby shampoo that lingered on her skin. Lily must have bathed her.

As he straightened, another scent—something soft and feminine, with a hint of something fruity—hit his nose. His breath caught. Lily smelled wonderful, too.

Probably would be better if he didn't know that...

After a long pause, Lily said, "Be right back."

He nodded, hoping he looked as if he hadn't just discovered how great she smelled. She went one way and he went the other as he continued on into the kitchen to wait.

He stopped dead in the doorway. The small table had been covered in a navy blue tablecloth he'd bought for the one dinner he'd attempted to host for Anna, Jim and Fran, and was simply set. Several covered dishes sat on the counter, awaiting serving.

Though it was a basic setup, something people came home to all the time, an odd kind of melancholy filtered through him. He couldn't remember the last time he'd come home to a waiting meal and a table ready for him. And that was a gloomy fact when he really thought about it.

He was beyond grateful for what Lily had done for him, though, and he wouldn't dream of letting on about the peculiar sadness her handiwork had brought on. So he focused on getting the beverages poured and on the table.

Lily returned in a few minutes. "She's one with her crib." She had a burp cloth over her shoulder and Blake thought it was one of the most appealing accessories he'd ever seen.

Put off-kilter by that strange notion, he did his best to keep his voice even. "Given how much time I've spent trying to get her to sleep, I should be happy she was snoozing when I got home."

She started uncovering the food. "But… you're not happy?"

"Just a bit disappointed." He let out a sound of self-derision. "Weird, I know, but I was really looking forward to spending some time with her."

"That's not weird at all. And I actually considered trying to keep her awake until you got home."

"No, you did the right thing."

"Thanks." She looked the table over. "So you're all set. Anything I can get you before I head out?"

He dropped his chin, feeling like an idiot. He'd thought she was staying to eat with him. "Um…" He darted his gaze to the table, hoping it appeared as if he were just looking the table over, to confirm she wasn't staying. One plate, not two. How had he not noticed that? "No, no, everything looks fine."

"Great!" she said, grabbing her purse from the counter and then hefting her briefcase onto one arm. "I'll be back in the morning at eight."

"That sounds perfect," he said.

"Okay, then, see you then." She moved toward the hall and turned. "Oh, I made a few extra bottles for you to use later and left them in the fridge. I know it's no fun making those things in the middle of the night."

Lily seemed to think of everything.

"I gave her fever reliever right before she went down, so if she wakes up again, you can give her another dose before bed. Otherwise just let her sleep."

"Got it."

Lily gave a little wave. "Bye."

"Um, Lily?"

"Yes?"

"You might want to lose the burp cloth," he said, fighting not to grin.

Her gaze went down to her shoulder and she rolled her eyes. "Oh, man, what a space cadet." She yanked the cloth off. "I would have left that thing on for the rest of the night."

"I decided to take pity on you and give you a heads-up." He held out a hand. "I'll take it."

She put the cloth in his hand. "Thank you. Knowing Molly, she probably would have let me wear it around for quite a while."

"Are you guys getting together tonight?" he asked, giving voice to his curiosity about Lily's social life.

"Yeah, she and Grant wanted to set me up with some new guy in town." Lily shook her head and gave a little snuffle. "They think I need to be dating, but I'm not interested, so I told Molly no to the setup and will be just meeting them instead. Molly and I are planning the annual singles' group Valentine's dance, so we'll probably talk about that."

An odd kind of relief had Blake's shoulders relaxing a bit. "So no dating for you?" he asked, more curious than he should be about what she had to say.

"I'm not interested in any kind of relationship right now. I need to focus on my career goals, not falling in love."

Made perfect sense, though for some reason her statement had disappointment poking at him. He shook the emotion off. "I hear you there," he replied. "Who has time for romantic relationships?" Or the guts.

"Not me."

"Not me, either. I have more than I can handle with the store and Peyton."

"So you aren't interested in dating, either?" she asked in what seemed like a very well-modulated voice.

"No," he said emphatically. "I don't have time." Which was part of his reasoning. The other part was too personal to share. Besides, he was sure she wouldn't be interested in his beliefs about the hazards of love.

"Right? Me, neither." She hesitated, her brow creasing in a pensive way. "We're actually a lot alike, you know."

"Hmm." The more he got to know her, the more he realized how true that was. He nodded, canting his head. "You know, you're right."

"Maybe that's why we get along so well."

"That has to be it," he said. "We're on the same page."

"Right." She nodded. "Same page is good. Really good."

"Actually, it's excellent. We get each other."

"Yes, we do," she said, her gaze meeting his. It held. Something passed between them; what, exactly, he couldn't say, just something odd yet exciting, something that made his heart pound. Then, after a beat of time that seemed too short yet too long, her gaze skittered away.

Taking her cue, he looked at his feet, and save for the sound of his heart beating in his head, silence reigned for a long, awkward moment.

"Well," he said, filling in the quiet.

She said, "I gotta jet," at the exact same moment.

More awkwardness. He set it right. "See you tomorrow." He waved.

"Yes, at eight sharp." She waved back, gaily it seemed. "Bye."

"Bye." He put his hands in his pockets and stood there, and a few moments later he heard the front door open and close, and then he was by himself.

He let out a breath and then regarded the meal she'd made him—hamburgers, steamed carrots and apples, along with what looked like instant pudding for dessert. It looked delicious. Better than anything he would have ever put together.

But it also looked like exactly what it was: a meal he would be eating alone with nothing but an unwanted sense of foolishness for thinking that she was going to stick around and eat with him.

And regret for letting himself be even mildly disappointed when she'd told him she was perhaps less interested in finding love than he was.

Chapter Five

◝❧

Lily threw her portfolio into the trunk and quickly got into her car, shut the door and locked it. Her hands went to the steering wheel and she leaned on it, her head down, taking shaky breaths.

Rapid-fire questions bounced around in her head. How had a discussion about a burp cloth, of all things, morphed into dual I-don't-have-time-for-love confessions between her and Blake? How—and why—had she even let the conversation even go that way? Not exactly impersonal discussion between her and her employer. In fact, the exact opposite, just what she didn't want. Figuring out they had so many things in common had made her feel connected to him. She wanted to remain *un*connected.

Well, she'd blown that. Majorly.

Good thing she had a dinner with Molly and Grant, or Lily might have stayed to partake with Blake.

Another question nagged at her. Had she been imagining the disappointment on Blake's face when he'd figured out she wasn't staying to eat? Yeah, she had to have imagined that. Why would he care one way or another? She was his daughter's babysitter. Not girlfriend material, if he were looking for one. Which, by his own admission, he wasn't.

She lifted her head and squared her shoulders. Excellent. Couldn't be better. They had the same goal—to focus on other things rather than finding love. It was the perfect setup, one that would allow her to make money for the time being and not be distracted from making sure she got on *Project Fashion*. She couldn't blow the deal by letting herself get hung up on Blake. No way. She wanted to move to LA and be on that TV show, and nothing was going to detour her from that goal ever again. Not even a great guy like Blake.

Feeling more resolute, and more focused on what she wanted, she drove home to change before she met Molly for dinner. Somehow she didn't think spit-up was a good fashion statement.

The sun had set and the western sky was

streaked with the last remnants of pink, red and orange. Maybe it would be sunny tomorrow. Although Lily wasn't holding her breath. As a native Washingtonian, and a coaster at that, she knew better than to wish for sun over rain very often.

The house Lily had grown up in was one of the older ones in Moonlight Cove, set on a large lot on the east side of town, at the end of Crab Leg Lane. It was a classic '30s bungalow-style home, and had white siding and black windows and shutters. She and Mom did their best to keep the house in good repair, but the budget didn't allow for all of the necessary maintenance, and the house was showing signs of shabbiness.

Dad had loved working in the yard, and when he was alive, the landscaping had been pristine and abundant all year long. Neither she nor Mom had the time—or inclination— to keep the yard up in the same way he had, and it had fallen into a state of bareness and neglect that Dad would have hated.

Still, Lily loved the house; it had a worn familiarity she was going to miss.

After she parked in the driveway, she hustled up the concrete stairs to the narrow porch. The screen door hung open on a broken hinge, and she made a mental note to stop at the hardware store sometime in the next few days to get a new hinge. Hopefully she could figure out a way to install it. She wasn't at all handy, and Mom was, if possible, even less of a handy-woman. It was like the blind leading the blind when it came to repairs around here, and they usually just did their best and hoped every-thing held together. It was a wonder something major hadn't fallen down.

She went inside and found her mom hover-ing around the tiny entryway as if she'd been waiting for Lily. Mom had her hip-length, gray-streaked dark hair pulled back into its customary ponytail and she wore old jeans and a red sweater that had seen better days. She wore no makeup, per usual, and the lines in her face seemed even more pronounced today than they usually did. Her large, '80s-style glasses perched on the bridge of her nose.

Mom was a no-nonsense woman who didn't spend any time on what she called frivolities. Though she wasn't unattractive, she was def-initely careworn. She worked hard six days a week and spent little time on herself.

Lily thought a tiny bit of tasteful makeup, some new clothes and an occasional trip to the local hairdresser would do wonders, but Mom refused to hear of it, saying she didn't have the time, money or inclination. Lily always dropped the subject. To each his own.

Lily put her keys on the small table in the entryway. "Hey, Mom. Were you waiting for me?"

Mom put her hands in her back pockets and sidled around. "Yes, I was."

A jolt of concern hit Lily. "Is something wrong?"

"Not exactly wrong," Mom said. "I just need to talk to you."

Lily frowned. Odd. Mom wasn't a big talker, and she never seemed to need a confidante. She was very self-sufficient. "O-okay," Lily said. "What's up?"

"An odd thing happened at the supermarket today." Mom worked at the Moonlight Cove Food Way three days a week.

"What was it?"

Mom drew her eyebrows together, then shoved her glasses up her nose. "Well, Lionel Shaver came in like he does every morning, and got his doughnut and coffee." She manned the bakery most mornings, then moved to the cash register after lunch.

"Okay." Where was this going? Lionel Shaver was the local plumbing contractor, and had lived in town for as long as Lily could re-member. He was in his fifties, probably, and if she remembered right, his wife had died of cancer a few years back.

"And, well, the strangest thing happened when he picked out his doughnut." She shook her head. "He actually asked me out."

Lily blinked. *"On a date?"* Since Daddy died, Mom had never so much as said the word *date*, much less expressed interest in a man. Any man. Having a social life—or a romance—was definitely not on her radar. Lily was certain her mom would go to her grave a widow who still carried a torch for her beloved dead husband.

"That's what I thought," Mom said, her tone incredulous. "Why would he want to go out with me?"

Lily wished she could call her words back. "I didn't mean it like that."

"Well, *I* did." Mom gestured to her head. "Look at me. I'm not exactly the prettiest flower in the bunch." Lily was quite sure on some subconscious level her mom hid behind baggy clothes, long, graying hair and large glasses that seemed to be permanently attached to her face. Mom might as well be wearing a sign that said Men, Do Not Approach.

"That's not true." Lily remembered her mom as a vibrant, outgoing, gorgeous younger woman with a quick wit, kind heart and beautiful face. She'd only gone shields up since Daddy had died.

Mom waved a hand in the air. "Oh, come on, honey. I'm a fifty-four-year-old widow who works two jobs and hasn't been to the hairdresser since Clinton was president."

"True, but you have good bones, and you're friendly and helpful."

Mom crooked one side of her mouth up. "You make me sound like a dog."

Lily was horrified. "What I meant was—"

"I know what you meant." She grabbed her baggy sweater and shook it. "That underneath all of this there's a reasonably attractive woman?"

"A gorgeous woman," Lily said honestly. She'd seen that woman. "One who's been hiding for a long time."

Mom sat down on the plaid couch that had been in the living room since before Lily's birth. "What do you mean 'hiding'?" She looked genuinely perplexed.

Lily sat next to her. "You really have no idea?"

"I'm clueless," Mom said, pulling her hair around and fiddling with the ends.

How best to put this? "First, you have to promise to hear me out, all right?"

Mom's brow creased. "Boy, it must be bad."

"Not bad." Lily shifted so she was facing her. "Just honest."

"Honest is good." Mom made a rolling motion in the air with her hand. "Just tell me."

"Well, this is just a theory, but I think you've let yourself go as a way to keep interested men at bay."

Mom's mouth went slack, but she kept quiet.

Lily pushed on. "Here's why I think that. You wear those big glasses, long hair and baggy, old clothes. To me, it seems like you're hiding behind all of those things as a way of protecting yourself."

"From?"

"From falling in love again and getting hurt."

Mom sat for a moment, chewing on her lower lip. "Losing your dad devastated me," she said in a husky whisper. "I came very close to completely breaking down."

"I know." Mom had been inconsolable for months after Daddy had died, and had become so skinny, Lily had thought she was going to blow away. Many nights Lily heard Mom crying in her bed for hours. Lily had never seen someone so lost, so completely flattened, and she'd vowed then never to be so dependent on a man she'd fall apart if he were suddenly gone.

Who would actually set themselves up for that kind of heart-tearing emotional agony?

Mom's lips quivered. "He was a wonderful man, and I loved him very much."

Lily's eyes burned. She let Mom go on.

"Losing him did make me wary of love. Petrified of it, actually. I really didn't think I'd survive it if I let myself love someone else and lost them, too." Her lips quivered. "A person can only take so much grief."

Lily's throat clogged. "Case in point, and one of the reasons I want to avoid falling in love."

For a moment, Mom sat, pensively silent. "I guess I feel the same way. I can't accept Lionel's invitation. Not yet. Maybe never."

Lily accepted her mom's statement at face value. Matters of the heart had no timetable. Especially where grief was concerned. But another idea popped into her head. "Fair enough. But how about a mini makeover?" She curled her right hand in and blew on her fingernails. "Fashion is my thing, you know."

Mom chuckled and straightened her sweater. "What, you don't like me frumpy?" she asked in a mock serious voice.

"I love you no matter how you are," Lily said, hugging her mom. "But a little update never hurt anyone."

Mom hugged her back. "You're right, of course." She pulled away and flipped her hair over her shoulder. "Maybe it is time to bring my look into the twenty-first century."

"Great!" Lily said, an idea taking shape in her head. "How about I design and make a few things for you?"

"Will you have time?"

"I will while Peyton naps, and in the evenings," Lily said.

"Sounds like a great idea." Mom's expression turned speculative. "How are things going with Peyton?"

"Fine." It would be better if she could manage to keep her distance from Peyton's daddy. Not that she'd spill that information. Lily preferred to keep her unwanted fascination with Blake from Mom; she was well aware that her mom fully supported Lily's plan to focus on her career instead of love. "Peyton still isn't feeling well, but she's sleeping now, which is good."

"It's never fun when babies don't sleep," Mom said. "Laura was a terrible sleeper."

"I remember," Lily said. "Blake is pulling his hair out over it. He's exhausted, and really has his hands full with Peyton and his store."

Mom raised a brow and looked at Lily, her brown eyes piercing. "So it's *Blake*?"

"What? You think I'm gonna call him Mr. Stonely?"

"Do I sense some interest there?" Mom said, ignoring the question.

"What?" Lily shook her head, hoping she appeared disinterested. "Why would you say that?"

"Because I know you, and I'm sensing—" Mom tilted her head to the side, her eyes narrowed as she trained an intense gaze on Lily, and then she circled her fingers in the air "—something."

Lily looked away from that penetrating stare. Mom had always been very intuitive. "There's nothing between Blake and me." She would make certain there never was.

"Are you sure?"

"Yes, I'm sure." A long gaze lock between her and Blake and a few giddy emotions on her part didn't count as anything.

"If you say so. But there's no denying Blake Stonely would be a catch."

Definitely. But not for Lily. "I don't want to catch a man." She lifted her chin, walking the walk. "This is just a job, nothing more."

"What about Peyton? Is it going to be hard not to get attached to her?"

Uneasiness crept into Lily and dug in surprisingly hard. "Probably. But I'll deal with that when the time comes."

"I'm sure you will," Mom said with a steady smile. "You're a strong person, and determined to make your dream come true. With so much at stake, I have faith you can keep everything under control and focus on your end goal."

Lily smiled, hoping she looked confident. "That's the plan." She simply needed to buckle down and make it so.

Chapter Six

Blake flipped off the lights of the store and stretched his neck from side to side as he headed out the back door to his car. It had been a long day, and he was more than ready to go home and see Peyton.

Though it was only the second day Lily had been babysitting, they had fallen into a good routine. She'd shown up this morning promptly; he'd handed over the reins to her and left for work. She'd called him with Peyton updates every two hours as they'd planned, and so far, the baby seemed to be feeling better. He could rest assured Peyton was in good hands. And, thankfully, Jonah was doing fine as the barista/backup server/all-around helper.

Blake's life was smoothing out, and he was beginning to think he'd been foolish for getting so stressed out when Mrs. Jones had called in sick and things had gone sideways. Now that Lily had taken over Peyton's care during the day, he could relax and focus on The Cabana.

God had undoubtedly had a hand in it all, and Blake said a prayer of thanks as he unlocked his car.

Everything was going to be okay.

Just as he sat down behind the wheel, his cell phone rang. He dug the phone out of his pocket and saw it was Lily calling. Hmm. Her two-hour check-in was a bit early...

He tapped Answer. "Hello?"

"Blake, it's Lily."

"You're a bit early."

"I know." She paused. "Um, I wanted to let you know that Peyton's fever is back up."

Worry zigzagged through him. "What is it?"

"It's 101.8."

"Oh, wow." He switched the phone to his other ear and started the engine. "It was almost normal this morning."

"It's been down all day, until about an hour ago."

"Should we be concerned?"

"Not necessarily, but I wanted to let you know ahead of time so you wouldn't be caught by surprise." Peyton cried near the phone. "She's not a very happy little girl at all."

"I can hear that."

"Yeah, she doesn't want to be put down. Ever. And she won't take her bottle, so I can't get her medicine in."

"Well, I'm on my way home," he said. "How are we doing on fever reducer?"

"Fine there."

Peyton let out another shrill cry.

"I'd better go and try to soothe her," Lily said.

"I'll be home in less than five minutes."

"Okay, bye."

"Bye." He hung up and put the car into gear, taming the impulse to gun it and speed out of the parking lot in back of the store. Peyton was being well taken care of. There was no need to break the law.

Even so, he drove quickly, anxious to get home and take stock of the situation with Peyton himself. The fever was stubbornly holding on, though it had seemed to wane earlier today, and he was now fairly concerned. Lily wouldn't have reported the fever and raised the alarm if she didn't think it was something to worry about.

So he worried. Peyton was so little, so vulnerable. Was her tiny body and infant immune system having a hard time fighting the virus off? What kind of toll would that take? What if the virus led to something serious? All kinds of dire questions bounced around in his brain, setting his nerves on an even harder edge as he made his way to Main Street.

Man, parenthood was nerve-racking. How did people manage taking care of kids without going completely insane? Sometimes he wondered if he wasn't cut out for the stress of parenting. He certainly hadn't had a good role model in his parents; his father had abandoned the family early on, and Mom had been strung out on drugs most of the time. Had their complete and utter inability to be good parents rubbed off on him somehow? Was it genetic? His hands tightened on the steering wheel.

He managed to keep under the speed limit as he navigated the car to the other side of Moonlight Cove, barely. As he headed down Main Street, which stretched from the north end of town to the south and was lined at its center with a quaint wooden boardwalk, his stomach felt as if he'd swallowed an orange. Or maybe a watermelon.

He saw a few tourists strolling down the boardwalk, just enjoying the day. Behind the buildings to his right, in the cloud-dotted sky above the beach, he saw a few kites riding the ever-present breeze, flown by those without any cares. What he wouldn't give for that kind of calm.

Within a few minutes Main Street took him to the south side of town. He hung a left on Mackeral Avenue and kept going for a few blocks, then veered onto Fogcutter Street. Second house in, he pulled into his driveway and drove under the carport. He shoved the car into Park and jumped from the vehicle instantly.

He kept the door leading from the garage to the kitchen locked, so he went to the front and let himself in. Piercing wails greeted him the moment he stepped into the house. Oh, boy. That didn't sound good.

He called out, so Lily would know he was in the house. "I'm home."

"In here," she replied back.

Following the sound of her voice—and Peyton's cries—he went to the kitchen. Lily's sketchbook had been abandoned on the dining table and she was swing-swing-swinging her heart out as she held a red-faced Peyton in her arms.

"Nothing seems to be working," Lily said.

He laid a hand on Peyton's forehead. "She still feels pretty warm."

"Yeah, she won't take the bottle." Lily adjusted Peyton in her arms. "I just tried again. No go."

He reached for Peyton. "Let me take her so

you can have a break." He doubted he could quiet her down if Lily couldn't, but he'd try.

Lily handed the baby over. "I'm a bit worried about her getting dehydrated." She took the burp cloth off her shoulder and laid it on his.

More anxiety chomped away at him. He swung Peyton up high onto his right shoulder. "Oh, I didn't think of that." Made sense, though. Peyton's only source of nutrition and hydration was formula given via her bottle.

"I don't think it's an immediate danger, but we have to keep it in mind, especially with her fever going up."

Peyton screamed and kicked her legs, her back stiffening. Was there anything more heartbreaking than a baby's distressed scream?

"Hey, hey, little girl. Shh. It's okay." He patted her tiny back and began the swing, swing, swing Lily had taught him. Then he started circling through the hallway to the living room and back to the kitchen. Around and around, walk and swing, walk and swing. He figured he'd traveled this route a hundred miles or so in the past couple of days. At this point, it seemed as if he'd be walking a hundred more tonight.

Lily loaded the dishwasher as he did his baby-quieting thing. After another few loops, she shifted to making dinner. As he walked by, he noticed her stylish skinny jeans and long-sleeved cream-colored top, which had some lacy stuff around the sleeves and collar. One of her own designs?

"You don't have to do that," he said as he circuited through the kitchen again. Maybe he was imagining it, but Peyton's cries seemed to be a bit less frantic.

"I know, but you're on baby duty and I need to stay busy."

He paused, then shifted Peyton onto her back and gently flipped her into the crook of his left arm. He resumed the swing. "Why don't you just head out. I'll get something to eat later." Or he'd fall into bed, exhausted. If he ever managed to get Peyton to stop crying. Just the thought of another long, sleepless night spent walking the dark hallways by himself, Peyton crying in his arms, filled him with dread. How long could he go without actual sleep and still function?

Lily opened the fridge and bent down to get something from the crisper. "I don't really feel right leaving while she's in this state."

"Oh." Her offer was unexpected, but, he realized, welcome. Four hands were better than two.

She was silent for a second, then rose a little bit and looked over the open fridge door, unblinking. "Do you mind if I stay?"

"No, not at all," he said quickly. "I just don't want you to feel obligated to." As he spoke, he realized the tenor of Peyton's cries had changed slightly. He looked at her and, yes, she did seem as if she was relaxing just a bit...

"I don't feel obligated at all." Lily closed the fridge and put a head of lettuce on the counter. Then she came over and gazed at Peyton with soft eyes. "I've grown pretty fond of this little peanut, and I'd like to stay and make sure she's okay."

Her dedication to Peyton lit a small but unmistakable fire in his heart. "Actually, it would be a big relief for me to have you here. I still don't really know what I'm doing."

Just then, Peyton hiccuped, let out a little cry, and then, after a few more short gulping sounds, her wails began to taper off. Her body relaxed against his arm just a bit, and her legs settled down.

He swung a questioning gaze up to Lily. Was it possible he'd actually gotten Peyton to relax?

Lily nodded quickly and made a rolling motion with her hand. Keep going.

Right. He resumed the swing and walk, retracing his route down the hallway into the living room and then back to the kitchen. And around again. With every loop, Peyton calmed more and more, and on the fifth or sixth circuit, she'd stopped crying completely and had begun to drift off.

Lily twirled a finger in the air and mouthed, "Don't stop."

So he kept moving, around and around, until Peyton had fallen dead sound asleep.

Triumphant, he went into the kitchen.

Lily was at the sink, washing lettuce.

"Should I put her down?" he whispered.

"I wouldn't risk it," she said. "Why don't you hold her while I eat, and then we'll switch and you can eat."

"Sounds like a plan."

Careful not to move too quickly and wake Peyton, he sat down at the table, which Lily had set with two place settings and the leftover burgers and fixings, along with salad and potato chips.

He raised his eyes and watched her fill two glasses with ice and water. Then she brought both over, put them on the table and sat in the chair opposite him. "Do you need anything else?"

He made a show of looking over the food on the table. "I was hoping for pudding again tonight," he joked.

She grimaced. "Sorry. I ate the rest of it,"

she said, a hint of guilt in her voice. "I kind of have a thing for chocolate pudding."

"Me, too."

"I was going to make more, but then Peyton woke up and started fussing, and my pudding plans went down the drain."

Her cute terminology made him grin. "Pudding plans?"

"Are you mocking me?" she asked with a lift of one eyebrow. But she was smiling the tiniest bit.

"No, ma'am," he deadpanned. "Pudding plans, well, those should never be mocked."

She pressed her lips into a straight line and lowered her chin, clearly trying to mimic his serious tone. "Of course not."

He looked at her, trying to return her somber expression. But it was useless. A laugh burst from him at the same moment she giggled. He let himself chuckle, and, man, did it feel good. He couldn't remember the last time he'd chortled with someone over something silly. After the day he'd had, it felt good to joke around, let down his guard. He relaxed back into his chair and looked down at Peyton as she slept away in his arms. Something tight wound around his heart and pulled.

Lily stared at him for a moment, then

grabbed a napkin and put it on her lap. "All joking aside, do you need anything else?"

"No, this is fine," he said truthfully. A sleeping baby. Good company. It was all good. "Go ahead and eat."

"Okay." She started putting a burger together and he covertly watched her, noting the copper highlights in her hair, wondering if it was as soft as it looked. Would it smell as good as she did?

He hastily veered himself away from that thought and instead analyzed another pressing matter at hand: Why was he letting himself be so drawn in by Lily? What was it about her? Why did he feel so content when she was around? Maybe the answer was simple.

It was nice to be taken care of.

He backed off from that idea. He didn't expect a woman—or anyone—to look after him. With his mother gone for days at a time during his childhood, he and Anna had learned to be self-sufficient early on.

But having Lily handle even small things while he dealt with Peyton gave him a sense of support as well as a welcome reprieve from the grind of being a single dad.

Thoughts of having a wife someday sneaked into his mind. Someone to grow old with. Someone to love, care for, and someone who would lend support on days like today. Was that just a dream, something for other people but not for him?

Just the thought of setting himself up to be vulnerable had his belly lurching. As Amy had taught him when she'd dumped him, love just involved too much risk. No way to get around that.

So he would enjoy Lily helping out for now. No harm in that. He would just have to be sure he didn't get used to depending on her; she'd be gone to LA before he knew it and he'd be back on his own. And alone all over again.

That was just the way things had to be in order to protect his heart and stay in complete control of his life.

"She's burning up," Blake announced from where he held Peyton on the couch in the living room.

Lily hustled over and put a hand on Peyton's forehead. Hot—really hot—to the touch. "Wow. Her temp has spiked." Worry zinged through Lily but she tried to remain outwardly calm; the last thing Blake needed was for her to panic. "Um…we should probably call Dr. Petrie." Doc Petrie had been the main pediatrician in Moonlight Cove since Lily was a kid and he'd been her doctor.

Blake nodded. "Yeah. He said to call if it went over 103." Blake had called Doc an hour ago, after dinner, just to be on the safe side.

"I'm not sure it's that high, but we should definitely check so we can give him all the information," Lily said briskly, attempting to stay in control and not let worry get the best of her. Blake needed her to be calm and collected. So did Peyton.

Blake blanched. "I hate taking her temperature."

Lily went for the digital thermometer on the counter. "Don't worry. I'll do it."

A few tense minutes later, they had their answer. "103.3," Lily said, her tummy sinking. "We need to call and figure out what to do next."

Blake already had his phone out. "On it."

Her heart pounding, Lily held a limp Peyton, almost positive Doc was going to tell them to take her to the emergency room. But it was important to get the go-ahead. Thankfully Lily was pretty sure Doc would answer his cell phone after hours—one of the perks of small-town medicine.

Sure enough, after a short wait, he picked up and Blake immediately went into what was going on. Lily held the baby close, feeling the heat emanating from Peyton. At one point in the conversation, Blake went pale himself at something Doc had said. After a few more seconds, Blake said, "All right, Doc. See you there."

Lily knew what "there" meant. The ER. The hospital.

Ribbons of dismay fluttered through her and she wavered for a moment. She hated the hospital. But now wasn't the time to let her memories of Daddy's last days take over. So before Blake had even hung up, she was up on her feet with Peyton in her arms, looking for the diaper bag.

She would be strong. It had been a long time since she'd been to the hospital. Surely the memories had faded.

"We need to go to the ER," Blake said just as she got her free hand on the bag. "Doc is going to meet us there."

She swung her gaze to Blake. He simply stood, shaking his head, his face waxen, his eyes radiating the tension that was clearly bubbling up inside.

She called upon her reserve of strength and composure. "It's going to be all right," she said in an even voice. "They'll figure out what's going on and they'll take care of her."

He reached out and took Peyton from Lily. His gaze dropped to the lethargic baby. "She looks completely drained." He rolled his lips in and blinked rapidly several times.

Lily's eyes burned in response.

"I almost wish she'd cry instead of this," he said in a husky voice.

"She's exhausted." And very sick. Trying to keep control, Lily mechanically swung the diaper bag over her shoulder and firmed her jaw. She had to focus on the plan of attack. "We need to get her to the hospital."

Blake lifted his head, then straightened his shoulders, as if he were preparing himself for battle. Which, unfortunately, he was. "Let me get my keys and we'll go."

"I'll meet you at the car," Lily said, donning her own mental battle armor as she headed outside.

The next few minutes passed in a blur as Lily and Blake got themselves and Peyton situated. But soon the baby was strapped into her car seat and Blake was backing out of the driveway like a shot.

Lily squelched a squeak of fear and widened her eyes.

He put the car in Drive and the wheels screeched as he straightened the car and took off.

Lily quickly gripped the granny handle and darted her gaze to him, noting that his shoulders were visibly hunched and his hands were so tight on the steering wheel his knuckles were white.

She reached out a hand and touched his arm. "Stop and take a deep breath."

"We have to get her to the hospital," he said, his jaw flexing, his hands opening and closing on the steering wheel.

"But we don't want to get in an accident or get pulled over on the way there," Lily said in an even tone. "What good would that do for Peyton?"

The car lurched to a stop and he shoved it into Park. "Okay, you're right." He let out a large gust of breath.

"Now relax your shoulders as you breathe out again."

He nodded and his shoulders went down.

"Now let your hands relax," she instructed.

His fingers gave up their death grip on the wheel.

"Great." She settled back. "The hospital is only a few minutes away. We'll get there quickly even if you don't speed."

"Okay," he said, swiping a hand over his face. "I'll relax and slow down."

"Thank you."

Traffic was light this time of night, and within five minutes Blake pulled the car into the emergency room parking lot and shoved the vehicle into Park.

"You get the baby. I'll get the diaper bag," Lily said as she exited the vehicle.

"Got her," Blake said, opening the back door.

Lily hurried by Blake's side into the hospital, almost running to keep up with his long, quick strides. She didn't complain. They were in emergency mode. Now that they were out of the car, fast was good.

The double doors whooshed open and she and Blake went through side by side. The second she was in the building, the hospital smell hit her and a shudder of revulsion ricocheted through her, stronger than she'd expected. Her quick steps faltered and all at once she was hurtled back fifteen years.

Daddy in the hospital. The grim prognosis. The rounds of chemo. Hope. More time here. Mom crying, fat tears streaming down her cheeks. Dad wasting away, sick, a shell of a man. And then him saying "no more." Their last time here, when they came to take him home.

He'd died a week later. In his own bed, where he wanted to be, with his family around him. But Lily had never forgotten that horrible time spent at this place. The sights. The smells. The sounds.

The numbing grief.

More loathing spread through her and she slowed even more until she almost stopped. She wanted to turn and run away. Hide. Never face this place again. She felt her breathing go shaky.

Blake turned, his gaze questioning. "You all right? You look pale." The fluorescent hospital light turned his hair to a washed-out shade of brown and his skin pasty. In his eyes she saw his fear, his worry, his need for support.

And then her gaze went to Peyton, lying limp in his arms, her skin like marble. A little baby statue.

They needed Lily.

She sucked in a big breath and slowly let it out. She could do this. "I'm fine," she said, moving forward, determined to be tough. There were more important things going on here than her bad memories.

Doc Petrie was waiting by the ER front desk. "I've already got you checked in and have a room ready," he said, adjusting his wire-framed glasses on his face. He pointed left. "This way."

Lily halted and flipped the diaper bag off

her shoulder and held it out to Blake. "Here, you might need this."

Blake halted abruptly and turned. "What?" He frowned. "You're coming with me."

"It's family only," she said, holding out the bag. She remembered a lot of things about how they ran things here.

He swung his gaze to Doc. "Doc, is it okay if Lily comes back?"

Doc waved her in as he held open the door. "I've known you since you were born. Come on back."

Lily started walking. "Okay."

"I would have had a huge problem if he'd said no," Blake muttered.

Lily suppressed a wisp of a smile and kept quiet. But she couldn't deny that it meant a lot to her that he wanted her there.

It felt very good to be needed. And to be able to face down her dread when the chips were down.

She followed Doc and Blake into the first curtained room on the right.

"Have a seat," Doc said. "Just hold Peyton for now."

Blake sat in the one ugly upholstered chair in the corner.

Lily hovered close.

An older nurse with short gray hair and

dressed in blue scrubs came in. "Hi, I'm Sylvia," she said. "What's going on with this little darling?"

Doc filled Sylvia in as he began to examine Peyton. Blake answered a few questions and then went silent as the exam continued. After a minute, he turned a hollow, despairing gaze to Lily.

A lump of dismay coagulated in her stomach. Even so, she gave his arm a reassuring squeeze. "It's going to be okay."

"I hope so," he said, his voice hitching in a way that tore her up inside.

Words wouldn't come to her, so she held out a hand and he took it, his warm grip tight.

Her hopes matched his. But hope didn't always bear out, as another stint in the hospital had taught her, and Peyton was clearly one very sick little girl. So Lily searched for her mental grit and did her best to communicate support with a firm, steady hold on Blake's hand.

Irrefutably, they were both going to need every bit of strength they could find if they were going to make it through the vital hours ahead without falling apart completely.

Chapter Seven

Half an hour later, Doc said, "So we'll keep her overnight to get her rehydrated and get her fever under control and we'll reassess in the morning." His hand rested on the rail of the hospital crib in which Peyton lay. "Clearly she's been hit very hard by this virus, and with her being so young, we really need to keep an eye on her."

A shudder of stark fear raked jagged fingers through Blake. Without thinking he reached sideways for Lily's hand. As her soft yet steady hand slid into his, he pressed his lips together and did his best to maintain control when all he really wanted to do was give in to the anxiety ripping him up inside and crumble inward. But he couldn't; Peyton needed him to be strong. *Lord, help me with that.*

"Can I stay here?" he asked.

"Of course," Doc said, adjusting Peyton's IV line. "The chair over there pulls out into a bed and you can spend the night."

Blake looked at the tubes running from Peyton to the fluid-filled bags hanging by the crib. What a nightmare. Thank goodness Peyton had fallen asleep a few minutes ago. She was undoubtedly exhausted by the trauma of the night, most particularly the IV insertion. She'd screamed bloody murder during that. Blake had almost cried himself, and even Lily, who seemed to be as strong as an ox regarding Peyton's illness, had looked upset.

"Would you like me to go to your house and get you some overnight essentials?" Lily asked.

Of course she would think of his needs. An unexpected ray of delight—and respect—shone through him. "No, I'll just sleep in my clothes and splash water on my face in the morning." Though he appreciated the offer, he didn't want to impose on Lily any more than he already had.

"I'll have Sylvia bring in a hygiene kit," Doc said. "It has a toothbrush and toothpaste and the like."

"Great," Blake said, realizing how ironic his response was. All of this was awful. But he had to take comfort in the fact that Peyton was exactly where she needed to be and would get excellent care. He'd hang on to that like a lifeline.

If he didn't, he'd never make it through the night without breaking down. Now that he thought about it, the sleeping situation probably didn't matter. He doubted he'd get any shut-eye at all.

Doc pointed toward the nurses' station. "Let me go get Sylvia so she can get you settled."

Blake nodded.

Doc left the room.

Lily squeezed Blake's hand. "How're you doing?"

"Not so good," he replied honestly, his gaze again going to Peyton looking so small and helpless in the crib. He felt so helpless, so powerless. Another facet of the nightmare this day had turned into.

"It was rough hearing her scream," Lily said.

He stroked Peyton's pale hand. "I've never heard her cry like that."

"All of my brothers and sisters had a fit like that when they got their shots."

"But hearing it, seeing it here tonight, still got to you?" he asked. Maybe it would make him feel better to know he wasn't alone in his feelings.

"Yeah, I guess I didn't hide it very well."

"I would think it was weird if you didn't

react. Her reaction was heartbreaking." He noted Lily's paleness and he brought his eyebrows together. "How are *you* doing?"

She chewed on her lower lip. "Honestly?"

"Of course."

"I don't really like hospitals." She firmed her lips and looked at the floor for a few moments. When she raised her head, her eyes shone with sadness. "Lots of bad memories."

For a second, he didn't know what she meant. Then it hit him. "Your dad."

She nodded. "Yeah, he spent a lot of time here."

"I should have realized..." He felt like a complete idiot for not having thought of how this hospital odyssey would affect Lily. Kudos to her for managing so well he hadn't even noticed her distress.

"No, you were focused on Peyton, not me. As it should be." Lily turned her attention to Peyton. "She needs you more than I do."

Her unselfish statement was a bright spot in what had been a long night of darkness. "I'm not sure what I would do if you weren't here."

Lily hesitated, and then her response was precluded by Sylvia coming into the room, a small ditty bag in her hands. "Here you go." She bustled into the en suite bathroom. "I'll just put it in here."

"Thank you." Suddenly he knew exactly what he and Lily needed. "Sylvia, are you going to be in here for a little bit?"

"You bet," Sylvia said. "This little angel is my only patient right now, so I'll stay." She went over to the computer station in the corner. "I have some record updating to do right here. The paperwork never ends."

"Would you mind if we took a break?"

"Actually, I encourage it," Sylvia said. "She's sleeping comfortably now, so you might as well take a breather while you can." She scrolled through a document onscreen. "Yes, I have your cell number. I promise to call if anything changes, or if Peyton wakes up."

"Thank you." Peyton would be in good hands, and they wouldn't be gone long. Blake looked at Lily. "Come with me."

"What? Where are we going?"

He crooked a thumb over his shoulder as he backed toward the door. "I have someone I need to talk to, and I need you to come with me."

Lily frowned, but followed him into the hall. "Who?"

"I'll show you. Just follow me."

After a short, silent elevator ride down to the first floor, he led her through the lobby, past the gift shop and down a short hallway. Soon they stood before the wooden door leading to the hospital chapel.

"I thought maybe we both needed a visit here," he said. He needed to pray, and maybe Lily did, too.

"Oh." She shifted on her feet and looked at the floor, studiously, it seemed, avoiding his gaze. "Hmm." She nodded stiffly. "The chapel."

He studied her, wondering about her odd demeanor. He cocked his head to the side. "Yes. I think we might find comfort here."

"O-okay." She chewed on the inside of her cheek. "Sure."

He considered her, trying to figure out what was going on. Maybe she wasn't a believer. "Are you not religious?"

Her face froze. "I used to be." One slim shoulder went up and then down. "But...I haven't been in a church since my dad died."

Shock rolled through him. "Oh. Okay." He hesitated, not sure how many questions to ask. But he had to know what was behind her statement. "Um, mind if I ask why?"

She shoved her hands in her jeans pockets. "I went to church as a kid. Every Sunday, in fact."

"So what happened?"

She grimaced. "Daddy got sick, and we

prayed and prayed that he would recover," Lily said in a low raspy voice. "Mom almost wore out her Bible as she searched for comfort, peace, faith, anything."

Suddenly Blake had a feeling he knew where this was going. And that realization made him feel ill. But he simply nodded and let Lily continue. This was her story to tell, though many of the tale's aspects were strangely familiar to him.

"Despite our prayers, Daddy never got better." Lily closed her eyes briefly and shook her head, as if she were reliving that time, moment by moment, as she spoke. "He wasted away, and then..." Her voice trailed off.

"And then?" Blake asked softly, his voice a bare whisper.

"And then our prayers changed," she said, looking right at him, her eyes devastatingly steady.

For a second Blake didn't understand. And then, in a blast of devastating comprehension, he got what she alluded to. And he wished he hadn't. He shook his head, unable to say the words, though he knew they were at the core of her story.

"After we knew he wasn't going to get better, we started to ask God to put Daddy out of his misery, to wrap him in His arms and take him quickly."

Exactly as Blake had thought. "But that didn't happen," he murmured.

She let out a quivering breath. "No. Daddy lingered, in agony, unable to eat or drink. He was just a shell of a man by then." Her eyes glittered with unshed tears, and Blake's burned, too.

She pressed shaky fingers to her mouth. "Do you know what it's like to walk into a room every day and hope that someone has gone to a better place, only to hope in the next breath that they're still with you?" she asked in a voice he'd never heard.

Words clogged Blake's throat. Her agony kicked him straight in the gut, and brought tears to his eyes and a tightness to his chest.

"And worse yet, that person is suffering, wasting away before your very eyes, and there's nothing you can do but wait for God to take them even as you feel guilty for hoping He doesn't?" she asked, pain evident in every syllable she spoke.

His breath caught as her ache socked him in the heart and became his. He took her hand. "No, I don't." He had experienced part of what she and her family had gone through, but not that part. "Awful. It must be awful."

"It truly was. We prayed to the Lord every single day and no matter what we prayed for, God didn't answer our prayers." Lily sniffed. "Mom vowed never to set foot in another church ever again." A single tear rose from one of Lily's eyes and trailed down her cheek.

Lily's story made unnerving sense, and it sounded achingly familiar. His next words weren't hard to find, though they would be difficult to say; he wasn't good at sharing, and what he was about to say would undoubtedly start a challenging conversation. But seeing her standing there, so upset, made him want to talk her pain away. "She felt as if God had let her down," he stated, wiping that tear away, feeling her silky, damp skin beneath his finger. "Abandoned her in her time of need."

Lily looked up at him, two lines forming between her eyebrows. "Yes, exactly." She blinked. "How...how did you know that?"

"Because I've recently had my own issues with God."

"You did?" Lily asked. "Tell me."

For a moment he hesitated as second thoughts poked at him. Was he really sure he wanted to share so much with her? Wasn't he trying to keep things impersonal between them? Did he really want to admit something he'd never divulged to anyone except Jim?

Blake had opened the door. Could he really step through and possibly take things to the next level?

He recalled how much Lily had done for him and Peyton. It seemed right to help Lily in any way he could. He owed her that. Perhaps he could offer some measure of comfort by letting her know he'd felt much the same way she had and he'd found a way to navigate through the doubts to come out the other side.

So he forced out, "Just a few weeks ago I thought God had abandoned me, too."

Lily blinked up at him. "No way."

"It's true." He shifted on his feet. "And I was so mad at Him I was sure I'd lost all of my faith in one fell swoop."

Blake's revelation sent shock waves through Lily and she fought to keep her jaw from sagging. "But your faith seems so strong."

"It is, now," he said. "But after Anna died, I was sure God had completely abandoned me."

"So you understand," she said, finding unexpected comfort in the bond they shared.

"I do. One of the people you loved most in life is gone forever, and you wonder why God didn't answer your prayers, why He ignored your pleas. You feel all alone." Blake regarded her. "But you're not alone."

She frowned.

"You don't believe me," Blake said.

"I just know how I felt—abandoned by God and alone with my grief." She chewed on her lip. "I can't just turn off those feelings because you say I should."

Blake blinked.

"I've offended you," she said, contrite.

His eyes went soft. "No, not at all. You're entitled to your feelings, no question. But let me just say that I've been where you are, and can attest that feelings change. Maybe yours can, too."

That sounded reasonable. "I guess this is a touchy subject for me."

"Faith is a very personal thing, and it ebbs and flows in everybody."

"Mine has been ebbing for a long time." A profound hollowness formed in her gut as she realized how far away she was from God.

"Maybe if you come in with me it will start flowing again."

Lily thought for a moment, feeling a push/pull inside. On the one hand, she wanted to support Blake. On the other, she was afraid to even approach the Lord. She hadn't had faith in Him…

"I think you might feel better if you prayed," Blake said. "Maybe it would be a good way to dip a toe into finding your way back to God."

"I'm still not sure where I stand with Him," she said, needing to be honest. What if He had forgotten her?

"God is there for everybody who seeks Him," Blake said solemnly. "Simple as that."

A lump grew in her throat. "Even when someone's faith has wavered?" She kept her eyes straight forward, afraid if she looked at Blake, she'd cry. And that surprised her. She'd thought she was okay without God. But now she wasn't so sure.

Was that a complication she wanted to deal with?

"Even then," Blake said. "He never forgets His children."

That statement had her eyes watering and tears welling. She was a mess. And now wasn't the time for that; Blake needed her to be strong and stand beside him. So she'd buck up and do that. The question of her faith wasn't going anywhere.

"I guess I do want to go in with you," she said.

"I'm glad," Blake replied, the lines around his mouth easing.

Blake pulled the swinging door open. "After you."

She went into the small chapel, which was empty and silent, lit only by muted overhead lights. After a brief pause and a deep breath, she headed to the front row of chairs and sat down near the small altar.

It felt weird to be back in God's presence.

Blake sat down next to her and a lot of his tension seemed to ease. After a moment of quiet, he said, "It feels good to be in here. Reassuring. Just what I needed." He clasped his hands together in front of himself.

Lily hadn't prayed for a long time, and folding her hands on her lap felt awkward. She closed her eyes and waited for Blake to speak.

He cleared his throat. "Dear Lord, in this time of crisis, Peyton needs You. Please watch over her and keep her in Your loving grace. She's so young, so vulnerable, so…small." Blake's voice broke on the last word.

Lily's chest tightened at the emotion in his plea. Clearly he was struggling with the turn of events—who wouldn't be? His little girl was sick and it probably felt as if his life were falling apart all over again. He'd lost his beloved sister and now he had to face a threat to his niece.

But he had God.

Blake cleared his throat and went on. "And, please, help me find comfort in Your power and support, and help me make the right decisions and be the father she needs right now, even though I'm terrified of the challenge that I'm faced with." He paused. "And last, help me take care of Peyton to the best of my ability, even when I'm overwhelmed by the task."

Lily nodded. An excellent prayer, full of all the right stuff. Surely Blake would feel better now. How fortunate he was to have God—

"And about Lily," Blake said, cutting off her thought.

Lily's breath caught. She sat stock-still, her eyes still closed.

"She's lost her way, and she needs You more than ever right now, though she's afraid to ask You for anything."

Lily's breathing turned shaky.

"Please keep her in Your sight, and I know You will welcome her back into Your arms when she's ready." Blake stopped for one significant beat. "Amen."

Somehow Lily managed to say a quivering, "Amen." Even as she said the word, she knew Blake had shown her so much tonight.

She'd missed God, missed being able to lean on Him.

Without saying a word, Blake rose. Lily followed suit and trailed him out of the chapel.

When they were in the hall, Blake turned as he headed to the lobby. "I feel better. Do you?"

She took stock of her emotions. "Yes, I do,"

she said in all candidness. "Thank you for bringing me here."

He gave her a sideways glance. "So you're not upset that I included you in my prayer?"

"No, not at all. In fact, listening to your prayer made me realize something important."

He raised his eyebrows. "What's that?"

"I realized that you were fortunate to be able to lean on God, and that, in turn, helped me to see that maybe I might be able to work my way back to doing that myself." She stopped when they reached the elevator. "How did you know just what I needed?" He seemed to be particularly in tune with her tonight, and that impression made her a bit uncomfortable. Okay, a lot uncomfortable. Was she letting herself get too caught up in Blake?

Just then, his cell phone rang, blaring through the silence of the hospital lobby like an unexpected fire alarm.

Lily's heart jumped.

He snapped his lips into a grim line as he snatched the device from his pocket and pressed Answer. "Hello?" he said, his tone intense. He listened for a moment, his head down, paling with every second that passed.

Lily held her breath. The elevator arrived and the doors opened. In unison, they stepped on.

Blake nodded tersely. "Okay, we're on our way up." The call ended and he turned to Lily.

"What's going on?" she asked, though she was pretty sure she knew.

"Peyton's fever's gone up to 104," he said in a voice rife with tension. "She's not getting better. She's getting worse."

Chapter Eight

With his heart in his throat, Blake burst into Peyton's room, Lily hot on his heels.

Doc Petrie stood bedside talking with Sylvia.

"What's going on, Doc?" Blake asked, his gaze landing on Peyton as he rushed to her side. She was awake, but was still pale and listless looking. Again, he wished she'd cry, flail, put up a stink, anything to show some spirit. Her lethargy scared him to death.

Without preamble, Doc said, "We were discussing why Peyton's fever is up."

"Why isn't it going down?" Blake asked, taking Peyton's tiny, hot hand in his.

"I'm not sure yet." Doc's brow creased. "It may just be that the virus hasn't run its course. It may be because she isn't adequately hydrated yet."

"Is it possible she has pneumonia?" Lily asked.

"Her lungs sound clear, so I don't think that's it." Doc moved over and consulted the computer. "And her white count is slightly elevated. So at this point I really think we're dealing with a particularly nasty virus."

Frustration bubbled through Blake. "What's the next step?" he asked.

"I think it's going to be a waiting game," Doc replied, adjusting his glasses. "We'll monitor her vitals and keep the fluids moving. If her fever isn't down in the morning, we'll reassess and maybe call a specialist in."

A specialist. Blake rubbed an unsteady hand over his face. "All right," he said, though the thought of waiting the whole night in this agonizing limbo would be torture. "Can I hold her?"

"Let Sylvia and me finish up here and then you can hold her as much as you want."

"Okay, thanks," Blake said.

Doc and Sylvia turned their attention to the computer screen.

Blake put his hands on his hips and looked at the ceiling, moving his head left and right, trying to ease the aching tension crimping his neck into knots. Though he had a feeling the only remedy for the tightness would be a full recovery for Peyton.

"I'll stay with you," Lily said, her eyes searching his face.

Her offer made him smile for a second; she was a truly caring woman. And having her here would be great. But he couldn't ask her to hang around. She'd already done enough. And he needed to learn to handle the challenges of parenting alone because that was his reality. And reality could never be ignored without paying a price. "You don't need to," he said. "I'll be fine." He hoped.

"I know you will." Lily's eyes sought out Peyton. "But I'd really like to stay. And it's not like I'm going to get any sleep at home worrying about her."

He thought about her reasoning. One side of him acknowledged again that he'd really like to have some moral support. But the other, more practical, guarded side reminded him that there were two good reasons he shouldn't agree to her offer—he didn't want to impose and he needed to learn to stand on his own.

And he couldn't ignore that part of him that wondered if letting Lily stay would eventually create more problems than it solved.

A sharp cry from Peyton brought him out

of his warring thoughts. He turned her way, concern lurching through him.

Peyton kicked her legs and reached out her arms, looking right at Lily, whimpering. Her message was clear.

"She wants you," he said.

"No, she just wants my hair," Lily said, flicking her hands through the dark strands.

"Your hair?"

"Yeah, she loves to play with it."

"I think you're downplaying why she wants you." Blake was sure Peyton's reaction was about more than hair. Lily was great with her. "She's obviously become attached to you."

"You think?" Lily asked with not a little incredulity shading her voice.

"Yes, I do," he said truthfully. "And it's a good thing. It means she likes you. And that makes sense. You've spent a lot of time with her lately." More, certainly, than he had. That belated insight dug in, hard, but he tried to ignore the sting. He was determined to make this all about Peyton, not his worries about not spending enough time with her. His guilt about leaving Peyton with a sitter wasn't the issue here, though he would eventually have to come to terms with it—all working parents did— and he was nothing if not pragmatic about the challenges of single fatherhood.

"Good point," Lily said, reaching out to take Peyton's flailing hand. "So…should I stay?"

Peyton's cries quieted a bit. Clearly Lily's presence comforted her.

The push/pull intensified inside of him. As he considered his options, he saw Peyton clutch at Lily's index finger, then grab a hold, as if to say, "Don't leave!"

The skirmish in his head quieted. How could he ignore that plea? Obviously Peyton wanted Lily here. So his decision was easy. "Some moral support *would* be good." *For now.* "You should stay, definitely."

"Okay, then, good." Lily stroked Peyton's cheek. "Hear that, sweet pea? I'm going to stay with you and your uncle Blake tonight."

Blake zeroed in on Peyton's face. "She's smiling," he said. He'd done the right thing for her. That was what mattered.

"I think you're right," Lily said, her lips curving up into a smile of her own. Her eyes lit up with muted yet unmistakable pleasure.

Blake's breath caught and he could barely look away.

Blake took Peyton's other hand in his, resting fairly easy in his decision to have Lily stay. Peyton's happiness and recovery were the most important thing right now. As long as he focused on those things, and didn't allow himself to get used to having Lily's support—which he knew was temporary—everything would be fine. For him.

A sobering thought hit him from left field. What about Peyton? How would she react when someone she was attached to just up and left down the line, out of her life in an instant? Because Lily's leaving was inevitable, and she didn't plan on returning. He'd be fooling himself if he believed otherwise.

And if there was one thing he never wanted to be again, it was a fool. Especially now that every decision he made not only affected him but an innocent child, too.

Lily startled awake from where she sat with her head back against the chair by the hospital room window. Oh! She hadn't meant to drift off. She looked at her watch. Five in the morning. She was an early riser and had been up since five yesterday morning; no wonder she'd dozed off.

She smoothed her hair back and rubbed her eyes, and then the sound of soft singing drifted to her. She turned her head left and saw Blake sitting next to Peyton's crib holding her high and close in the crook of his right arm. He'd bent his head low so he could sing in her ear and Peyton looked to be sleeping. At the very least, she was calm.

Lily froze, not wanting to disturb them. Or alert him to her observation. Her heart melted a bit at the sight of him holding the baby in his arms as if he were holding spun glass that might break at any moment. Her conversation with Molly at the singles' event came back to her. What was it about a guy who was good to kids? Why were they so attractive? So tempting? So very, very hard to ignore?

Suddenly it seemed very important that she figure out what that intangible thing was, exactly, so she could guard against the threat.

She furrowed her brow, and she listened intently, trying to hear the strains of the song he sang. Blake had a great baritone singing voice, soft yet expressive, and right on key.

She sat very, very still, entranced by the tenor of his voice. After a moment, she drew her eyebrows together. Was he singing "Whole Lotta Love"? She quit breathing for a few long seconds so she could hear better. Yes...yes, she wasn't mistaken. He was singing the Led Zeppelin favorite to Peyton.

Lily put her hand over her mouth and giggled under her breath.

Blake's gaze flew her way and he went quiet. "You're awake," he said in a hushed tone.

She rose, trying to keep a straight face. "Yeah, sorry I dozed off."

"No worries." He glanced down at Peyton. "She's out."

Lily stretched. "No wonder with her own personal concert." What would it be like to have Blake sing to her, Lily wondered, his clear, expressive voice soft and low? Just for her...

She cleared her throat, trying to focus on anything but the thought of Blake serenading her.

Attributing her suddenly quivery legs to standing after being asleep, she stepped closer. "Were you singing 'Whole Lotta Love' to her?" Lily asked, focusing on unimportant details to keep herself from dwelling on Blake singing to her.

"You heard."

"Yep. I heard," she said, trying to keep from chuckling. "An odd choice."

"I don't know any lullabies, and my brain is so fried right now, it's all I could come up with."

"She does seem to like rock. I sang some Journey to her yesterday, and it seemed to calm her right down."

He snapped his eyebrows together. "You a Journey fan?"

"Yeah, my dad loved them and I grew up listening to their music." She gave him a crooked grin. "My mashup of 'Don't Stop Believin'' and 'Wheel in the Sky' seems to be Miss Peyton's current favorite."

"She has good taste," Blake said with a small smile.

"Are you a fan of Journey, too?" Lily asked.

"I love all '70s rock."

Another commonality. Hmm. No biggie. "Who's your favorite band?"

He chewed on his bottom lip. "It's probably a tie between Boston and Aerosmith."

"That's a hard one to call." She leaned a hip against the in-room sink cabinet. "I'd have to go with Aerosmith, solely because of the song 'Dude (Looks Like a Lady).' I've always had a soft spot for that song."

"Good point." He adjusted Peyton slightly in his arms. "But Boston had amazing guitar and vocals."

"Yeah, but they didn't have Steven Tyler."

"True, true," Blake replied. "Hard not to like him."

"Right?"

A knock on the door sounded.

Lily went over and opened the door.

To her surprise, Doc Petrie stood there. He

wore rain-dotted street clothes. "Just me," he said.

She stepped back, holding a finger up to her lips. "Come on in," she said softly.

He followed her in and closed the door.

Blake turned. "You're here awfully early, Doc."

"I couldn't sleep thinking about Peyton, so I decided to just come in and see for myself how she's doing."

"We appreciate your concern," Blake said. "As you can see, she's settled down."

"That's good." Doc bent down to look more closely at Peyton. "Her color looks better."

"I thought so, too." Blake gazed down at Peyton, his lips pressed tight. "Hopefully that's a good sign."

The night had been agony for Blake, Lily knew. He'd alternated between pacing, drinking coffee, staring out the window, praying and holding Peyton. He must be absolutely exhausted, both mentally and physically.

Doc went to the computer and logged in. "Let's check her last temp, and then take it now and compare the two. That'll tell us a lot."

Lily went over and put her hand on the back of Blake's chair. Tension made her tummy tight and she figured Blake was surely feeling the same way—probably worse. Acting on pure instinct, she moved her hand to his shoulder and lightly squeezed, feeling the tenseness of his muscles beneath her touch. Somehow it was important she let him know he wasn't alone. That she was there for him and Peyton.

And touching him...well, that was...um, nice, too.

Blake stilled, then turned, his eyes zeroing in on her hand. He stared for a moment, his chin drawn in. Then his face relaxed and he turned and looked up at Lily, his eyes full of what appeared to be gratitude.

She simply nodded steadily, as if to say, "I'm here."

Doc pushed a few keys and brought up Peyton's chart, then leaned in, scrutinizing the data. He turned, his expression unreadable. "Well, at last check, the temp was still up over 104."

"Sylvia told me it was 104.3," Blake said.

Doc nodded. "Yes, that's right." He frowned slightly. "That's still pretty high."

Lily's stomach pitched and her hand tightened on Blake's shoulder.

Doc opened the cupboard over the sink. "Let's take it again and see where we are now."

Three endless minutes later, they had their answer.

"It's 101.6," Doc announced with a smile.

"Still over normal, obviously, but way, way down. It looks like maybe the virus has run its course."

Lily's nerves smoothed out.

Peyton let out a cry and Blake gathered her in his arms and held her close. "That's welcome news." Was that a tremor in his voice?

"Very welcome," Doc said with a smile. "We'll keep her for the morning, pushing the IV fluids, and then if her temp stays down, you can take her home around lunchtime."

Relief spread comforting fingers through Lily.

Blake looked up. "Thank You, God."

Automatically, Lily cast her eyes upward, a prayer of her own forming instantly. *Yes, thank You, Lord, for taking such good care of Peyton.*

As soon as the heartfelt prayer made its way out of Lily's brain, amazement hit her in a huge wave. Conscious thought usually stopped prayers in their tracks, and she hadn't prayed or asked God for anything since right before Daddy had died.

An amazing feeling of peace spread its way through her, and a profound thought rose in her head. It felt good to lean on God. Really good. Maybe she needed Him more than she'd thought.

But…how could she be sure the Lord would always be there for her?

Blake hit End on his cell phone and stopped pacing around his living room. He rubbed the bridge of his nose, trying to ease the ache that had sprung up there about an hour ago, right about the time he and Lily had brought Peyton home from the hospital. "That's the third call in the last forty-five minutes." Since leaving Peyton wasn't an option, he'd put Jonah in charge of running the shop. "He wanted to know how to open the blinds." Blake rolled his eyes.

Lily, with a snoozing Peyton in her arms, looked up at him. "He's probably really feeling the weight of responsibility."

"But blinds? It's not rocket science. Seems odd he can't handle it."

Lily rose and put Peyton in her crib. "True, but he has been slammed with a lot with no notice," she said as she moved closer. "And he's only worked there for a few days."

Contrition zapped Blake. "I guess you're right." He rubbed his gritty eyes. "No sleep's making me crabby. I hadn't thought of it from his point of view."

"Aren't I always right?" she asked, clearly joking.

"Actually, you *are* always right," he replied in a serious tone.

"My brothers and sisters would beg to disagree," she said with a wry quirk of her lips.

"No, I'm serious. You always manage to make me see things from a different perspective."

"That's because I'm not as close to the situation as you are." She shrugged. "I have the benefit of emotional distance."

"That's part of it, sure. But there's more." He let his gaze roam over her face, noting the gold flecks in her eyes and the very light freckles sprinkled across the bridge of her nose. Even with very little sleep, she looked beautiful. "You're very levelheaded, very good under pressure and quick to defend others."

Her face went an appealing shade of pink. "You flatter me."

"You need some flattery. You're a very selfless person, and I admire that."

She paused, then looked at the floor. When she looked back up, the blush had faded and a somber light had entered her gaze. "I appreciate the thought, really I do, but I actually consider my selflessness a flaw."

He scowled. "What?" That made no sense to him. "How can giving to others be a bad thing?"

She let out a heavy sigh. "I've spent most of

my life taking care of my brothers and sisters. Being selfless."

She went over to the window and looked out, her back to him. "For a good reason, obviously. My mom needed me. But I've always jumped in and helped no matter what."

"You sacrificed what you wanted." He was beginning to understand her so much better, and it fit with what he saw in her and in the way she'd waded in to help him with Peyton. She was selfless and giving to the extreme, but it had come at a big price to her. His heart cracked a little.

She turned, nodding. "Exactly. I've been bad at getting my own needs met. I've never been able to break away. To put myself first."

"But now…breaking away is going to happen," he said, finally comprehending why it was so important for her to go to LA to get on that reality show. "You get to do what you want to do, without anything holding you here." His words had a glob of sadness forming in the pit of his belly, but he tried not to analyze why too much. This wasn't about him or his reasons for wanting her to stick around Moonlight Cove.

And in reality, he wasn't ready to examine his own turbulent feelings about Lily. They were moot, anyway. She was going to say goodbye for good and he was happy for her.

Period. And in some ways, her plans should make it easier for him to keep her at arm's length as he'd planned. It would be ridiculously foolish for him to let himself fall for her knowing she was leaving.

He had to remember that, no matter how appealing she was.

"Exactly. I'm finally at a place where I can leave and do what *I* want for a change." She smoothed her hair back behind her ears. "I feel like my life is finally starting."

His chest went slightly hollow, but he shook the feeling off. She earned the right to follow her dream, so he'd be happy for her rather than sad for him and Peyton. "This is your time, and it's well deserved. Molly told me you design most of your own clothes, and though I'm no expert, you always look very stylish."

She smiled, her eyes glowing. "Thank you, I appreciate your support."

He could barely keep himself from staring at her pretty face. Instead, he focused on her nose. "It's the least I can do after you've helped me so much."

"Speaking of help, would you like me to go to The Cabana and help Jonah out?"

"You'd do that?" he asked, once again awestruck by her willingness to help wherever he needed it.

"Of course. You obviously don't need my help with Peyton, and you do need my help at the store." She put her hands in the pockets of her jeans. "I go where I'm needed."

"I know you do." And right now, he needed her and she was there. He liked that.

"Although, I can't promise I'll be able to handle everything at the store, I can promise a helping hand. And two brains are better than one, right?"

"Right," he said, grinning.

"Well, three if you count yours," she said, pointing to his head.

"I don't know if mine qualifies since I haven't slept for over twenty-four hours."

"Okay, so only two and a half brains," she quipped. "Still better than just one."

Her point, while made in a silly way, was well-taken. And he really didn't want to leave Peyton right now. It was practical to have Lily go to The Cabana. And it would put his mind at ease if she were there helping out. "Okay, I guess it makes sense for you to go help Jonah. I'll pay you, of course."

She saluted. "Aye aye, Captain Blake."

Her lighthearted demeanor had his stress level evening out. "How is it you always know how to make me feel better?" he said without thinking too much.

She blinked, clearly taken aback by his words, then recovered and returned his smile, though hers quivered in the corners. "Practice, I guess. I learned through long hours of trying to get four younger siblings on the same page without doing any bodily harm."

"Well, I'm grateful for it, more than I can really explain." She made his current challenges seem more bearable, less stressful and infinitely less threatening. She made life easier, and made him feel as if he could handle any challenge that came his way.

But—and there was always a *but*—she wouldn't be around forever, that was a given. Soon he'd be on his own again. Without her helping out, easing his load, making him smile. And he'd have no choice but to deal with the challenges of his life without her around to hold his hand.

And for the first time in a long time, he wished life could be different, that he could consider relinquishing control.

Chapter Nine

By the end of the afternoon spent helping Jonah at The Cabana, Lily felt energized. She'd been raised to work hard, and she liked the sense of accomplishment a job well-done gave her. It felt good to be helping, to be part of a team.

An hour before closing, while Lily manned the front counter, a face from the past came through the door. Louise Armstead, her short graying hair windswept, walked to the counter.

Lily had gone to high school with her daughter, Josie, and Lily and Josie had been good friends, their senior year in particular, when they'd been inseparable. Then they'd graduated and Josie had left town to go to school in Southern California while Lily had stayed behind to help Mom. Lily and Josie gradually lost touch. Last Lily had heard through the grapevine Josie was living in Seattle, working as a physical therapist.

Lily remembered Mrs. Armstead as a kind, practical, hardworking woman who had been heavily involved in the Moonlight Cove High School Parent Teacher Organization.

As Mrs. Armstead arrived at the counter, she looked up from digging her wallet out of her purse. "Oh, goodness me. Lily Rogers!"

"Hi, Mrs. Armstead." Lily gave a small wave.

Mrs. Armstead hesitated, her brow creased above her sparkling blue eyes. "I come here a lot, and I don't remember ever seeing you working here."

"Oh, I don't, actually. I'm just helping out the owner, Blake Stonely, today." She'd leave out why; it wasn't her place to tell people that Peyton was sick.

"Ah, I see." Mrs. Armstead put her purse on the counter and bestowed upon Lily a warm smile. "So, what have you been up to? I seem to remember you were working at the boutique around the corner."

Normally Lily would have launched into how she'd been helping out at home while working at The Clothes Horse, yada yada yada. And while all of that was, well, fine, her life was changing soon, and she wanted to start talking about how she envisioned her future as a clothing designer. And, really, it was time to let people in on her aspirations now that going to LA was becoming more of a reality. So she said, "Actually, I'm going to be moving to Los Angeles in a few months."

Mrs. Armstead's eyes lit up. "Oh, my, that's exciting. What's taking you down there?"

"I'm going to audition for the show *Project Fashion*."

"Really?" Mrs. Armstead said. "Oh, yes, I remember now you were always interested in fashion."

"Yes, Josie and I had a lot of fashion shows, didn't we?" Lily would design and sew, and Josie would model. A perfect partnership.

"I seem to remember you were quite talented."

Pride had Lily beaming. "Well, thank you. I've had the design bug for a long time." Ever since she'd started making clothes for her stuffed animals when she was eight.

"Doesn't surprise me at all." Mrs. Armstead's eyes lit up. "Did you know that Josie is engaged?"

"No, I didn't know that." Lily nodded, a grin on her face. Though inside, something curled inward. Most all of her friends from high school were either engaged or married.

Pretty soon she'd be the lone singleton. Why did that thought depress her so much? Shaking off the downheartedness creeping in, she said, "You must be thrilled. Congratulations!"

"Yes, I am. But I'm even more thrilled that she and her fiancé, whom she met while going to PT school in Oregon, are moving back to Moonlight Cove in just a few days to open their own physical therapy practice here."

"That's great. I'm sure you're ecstatic to have her back in town." Maybe it would be nice to reconnect with Josie. Although, would it be worthwhile since Lily was going to be gone by June? "When's the wedding?"

"In May," Mrs. Armstead said. "And all of the plans were coming along fine until the dress fiasco."

Lily's ears perked up. "Dress fiasco?"

"Yes, it's a total disaster. Someone at the bridal shop in Seattle messed up the order, including the bridesmaids' dresses, and now Josie is scrambling to find dresses on short notice. No luck there, and she's thinking of going off the rack."

A crazy idea grabbed a hold of Lily and wouldn't let go. For a second, she held back. But…maybe she should just go for it. So she said, "I've designed bridal dresses." Excitement laced her voice. She'd always wanted special occasion creations to be part of her line eventually, and she had tons of sketches in her portfolio and had many more bridal design concepts and themes swirling around in her head. "Any way I can help?"

Mrs. Armstead blinked. "Are you serious?"

"Dead," Lily said immediately. "It would be so cool to actually get to design and create the dresses for a whole bridal party. A dream come true, actually." Second only to getting on *Project Fashion.*

"Oh, wow." Mrs. Armstead tapped a finger on the counter. "Sounds like a great idea—I know how talented you are." She hesitated for a few long moments. "But Josie would have to agree, of course."

"Of course," Lily concurred, barely able to contain her enthusiasm. "The bride always has final say, no question. But I think it might be a really viable option."

"You'd do the sewing, too?" Mrs. Armstead asked.

"Well, yes," Lily replied, then reined herself in. Better to get details before she committed. "Um…how many bridesmaids are there?"

"Five."

Lily gulped. "So six dresses total?" That was a lot of dresses in a short amount of time. All while taking care of Peyton, at least until

Mrs. Jones came back. And who knew when that would be.

"Yes."

It would be a huge task, yes. But she wanted to do the work so badly she'd work night and day if need be. She shoved her doubts away. "Entirely feasible," she said, keeping a positive note in her voice to instill confidence in Mrs. Armstead.

Mrs. Armstead nodded. "It sounds like a real possibility." She bit her bottom lip. "But I'll have to check with Josie. Can I call you in a bit and let you know?"

"Of course." Lily grabbed a pad of paper sitting next to the cash register. "This is my cell number," she said as she wrote it down. "Call me and let me know what Josie says." She ripped the piece of paper off the pad and held it out to Mrs. Armstead. "If you and Josie want to do this, we'll need to get started sooner rather than later."

Mrs. Armstead took the paper and tucked it in her purse. "Josie is at her last day of work today, so I'll wait an hour or so to call her. Expect to hear from me this evening."

"Okay." Something else occurred to Lily. "And if you and Josie want to see my portfolio, that's totally fine. I could email some of my sketches if she wants to see examples of my work."

"I'll tell her." Mrs. Armstead sighed, then her face brightened. "I think you might be the answer to our prayers."

"I hope so," Lily said, holding back from actually begging for the job. Groveling wouldn't be professional.

But, oh, how she wanted this job! It would be a great addition to her portfolio, and would give her credentials that could prove invaluable to her career down the line. And they'd pay her; what a fantastic way to earn more money for her trip to LA.

Lily passed Mrs. Armstead's order on to Jonah. As anticipation bounced around inside of her like a Ping-Pong ball gone wild, she went out from behind the counter to the main part of the store to be sure all of the tables were clean, and then she checked the napkin dispensers. All good.

Mrs. Armstead said goodbye, to-go coffee cup in hand. Lily returned the sentiment, and, invigorated, she decided to tackle wiping all of the windowsills down. Anything to funnel her excitement into something productive.

Before she could go get the spray cleaner from the storeroom, reality came crashing down and her exhilaration deflated instantly.

She was taking care of Peyton full-time, and Lily's free time would be at a bare minimum and she wasn't sure it would be enough to design and produce six gowns for a complete wedding party. Again, genuine doubt overwhelmed her and her shoulders drooped, her upbeat mood taking a nosedive.

Her stomach clutched. Should she even tell Blake about the possibility of an offer from Josie? Lily dug her teeth into her top lip. She was pretty sure he'd understand—that was just the kind of guy he was—but she could be wrong.

But…there was no need for Lily to get ahead of herself, or buy trouble. Maybe Josie wouldn't be interested in a no-name designer. Maybe none of it would work out and the question of Lily having enough time to design and make six dresses wouldn't even be an issue.

But there was no denying that she wanted to do the work very, very badly and would be beyond disappointed if it didn't work out.

That night, Blake got Peyton to go to bed shortly after he wolfed down a late dinner. For the first time in forever the house was quiet, the baby was blessedly sound asleep and he had some precious time to catch up on household details.

As he sat on the couch with his laptop, still trying to design the flyer for the promotional offer, he bent his head and thanked God for the reprieve and for Peyton's further recovery. He looked up and also thanked the Lord for Lily. Blake honestly didn't know how he would have managed the past few days without her. She'd helped with Peyton, stayed with him at the hospital and taken over at The Cabana today. She was truly a godsend, and just the thought of her leaving town sent shards of panic through his system.

Why was that? Mrs. Jones would be back eventually, and he could pay her extra to do the chores Lily had been doing. In all reality, all of his child care and household needs would be met just fine when Lily wasn't around anymore. So why was he stressing over her leaving? What was so different about her?

The answer was no small comfort. He liked everything about her, from her caring heart to her tenderness with Peyton to her uncanny ability to make him feel as if any crisis could be handled. Mrs. Jones did fine with Peyton, and was loving and caring for sure. But Lily... Lily seemed to go above and beyond with everything she did.

Liking Lily so much scared him all the way down to the soles of his feet. He'd been abandoned by his mom and dad, and by Anna in death. Putting his heart on the line was a risk he didn't want to take again. No way. So what was he going to do about his feelings for Lily?

Nothing, he decided. So he was infatuated with her. Those feelings would pass as soon as he wasn't seeing her every day.

As exhaustion and anxiety dogged him, he eyed his open laptop. He should keep working on the flyer, but right now he just needed to relax. So, he decided to do something he hadn't done in a long time—simply sit down and watch his favorite baseball team, the Seattle Mariners, play.

Just as he got his feet up and the TV on the right station, his cell phone vibrated. Figured. He muted the TV and pulled his cell out of his pocket. Lily calling. Odd. She'd touched base just a half an hour ago and told him she was heading home from The Cabana. "Lily." He cleared his throat. "Everything okay?"

"Oh, yeah. Fine." She chuckled. "I hope you don't mind, but I, um, well, I was on my way home, and I decided to just stop by and check on Peyton for myself."

"Oh, okay, sure." He was careful to keep his voice neutral, despite his suddenly uneven heartbeat.

"I'm at your front door," she said, a sheepish tone coating her voice.

He flipped his feet to the ground and quickly rose. "Why didn't you just knock?"

"I didn't want to disturb Peyton."

Good call. She was smart that way. "Oh, okay." He headed toward the front entry next to the living room. "Be right there."

He opened the door and there she stood, her cell phone to her ear. Her hair was pulled back in a loose ponytail and she wore the same jeans and sweater she'd had on when she'd left the hospital this morning.

She smiled and looked as pretty as always. But truth be told, her smile held a touch of weariness. No surprise. She'd been up most of the night, too, and had undoubtedly had a full day at The Cabana.

"Hey, there," she said, clicking her phone off. "Hope it's not too late."

He gestured her in. "No, not at all." Would he ever not be happy to see her? Soon he'd have no choice in the matter. She'd disappear from his life and he'd have to live with it whether he liked it or not.

"I kept thinking about Peyton in that hospital bed, and I really wanted to see her." Lily walked past him, bringing with her the scent of wind and rain and her. "How's she doing?"

Had he ever smelled anything so wonderful, or met a woman so full of compassion and good intentions? She was truly one of a kind, and he had the sudden urge to hug her close.

He closed his eyes and summoned up his control as he pushed the door shut. "Well, believe it or not, Miss Peyton is actually asleep."

Lily turned, her eyes wide. "Get out."

He held up his hands, palms out. "What can I say? I learned from the best. I swung, swung, swung, and voilà, she went to sleep in ten minutes."

"Great." She let her purse drop to the floor.

Did it seem as if she were avoiding his gaze?

"You must be so glad to have some peace and quiet after the couple of days you've had," she said. "And that Peyton is doing so much better."

"Yes, I am." He rubbed his eyes. "I feel as if I've aged ten years over the last few days."

"Me, too."

An idea floated into his mind. "I was just sitting down to watch the Mariners play the Dodgers." He tried to catch her eye. "You like baseball?"

"I'm a fan of the game, yes," she replied. "My dad loved it. He grew up in Chicago, so the Cubs were his team."

"Ooh." Blake shook his head. "Is that a family tradition?"

"Maybe." She pursed her lips. "Why?"

"Because if it is we might have a conflict of interest on our hands," he teased, anxious to see her smile.

No smile. Just a frown. "Really?"

He cocked his head to the side. "No, I was just giving you a hard time."

"Oh." She smiled, but it looked fake, and it didn't reach her eyes. "Okay."

"Is everything all right? You seem tense." Distracted. Cagey. Unsettled.

She sighed, then hesitated for a few long seconds. "Actually, I need to talk to you."

Oh, boy. "Should I be worried?"

"I guess that'll be for you to decide."

Definitely a nonanswer. He held back a grimace, trying to hold on to his patience, and gestured to the couch. "Let's sit down and talk," he suggested, wondering what was on her mind. Was she sick? "Can I get you anything to drink?" he asked, minding his manners as Jim had taught him.

"No, I'm fine," she said, unbuttoning her coat, then sliding it off, sounding anything but okay.

As tension mushroomed inside of him, he took the coat and laid it over the arm of the love seat. He went over and sat next to Lily on the couch, careful to keep his distance. He had a feeling he was going to need his wits about him, and getting too close to Lily tended to scramble his brain. In a good way, if there were such a thing.

"So, what's going on?" he asked, zeroing in on her face, adopting his listening position. He wanted her to feel comfortable talking to him.

Her eyes caught and held on his open laptop. "What are you designing?"

He snorted. "A flyer. But my design skills are questionable."

"Mind if I take a look?"

"Be my guest," he said, gesturing to the computer.

With the laptop balanced on her knees, she looked over his design, her lower lip pulled between her teeth. "Well, you've got a decent start."

She was being kind. "I need to finish the thing as soon as possible."

"Mind if I tweak it a bit?"

"I'd love it, but I don't want to take up your time with my stuff."

"I'm a designer. It won't take long."

"It took me three hours to come up with that."

She grinned. "I won't hold that against you."

Her sassy attitude had him smiling back. "You sure?"

"Positive."

"Then have at it," he said, capitulating. "Can I at least get you something to drink?"

"That sounds good."

"I've got a hankering for some popcorn. You want some?"

"I love popcorn, so yes."

"Coming right up."

He banged around the kitchen getting everything ready and soon he was heading back into the living room with a big bowl of buttery popped corn and two refreshing colas.

She smiled when he sat down next to her. "Oooh, yes. I'm starving."

"Eat up," he said, throwing a piece of popcorn in the air and catching it with his upturned mouth.

A giggle escaped from her as she put the laptop onto the coffee table. "Yum," she said, taking a big handful.

His eyes strayed to the computer and his jaw slackened. In the few minutes he'd been in the kitchen, she'd turned the flyer design from yuck to *yes!* "That's amazing."

"Thanks. I just made a few adjustment to the spacing, the colors and the word placement."

"In other words, you fixed my mess."

"It wasn't a mess."

"Don't worry—I won't be offended by the truth."

"Okay, it was a bit of a mess. But the basic idea was on the right track. I just helped it all come together."

"You certainly did," he said, amazed by her design skill. "And I thank you. I've been pulling my hair out trying to get it right."

"Glad to help."

"So, as I asked before we were distracted by my messy flyer, what's on your mind?"

She grabbed one of the napkins he'd brought with the popcorn. "Maybe nothing, and I debated even telling you. But I can't in good conscience not let you know about what happened today."

Her words had him troubled—had something bad occurred at the store?—but he was determined not to react or interrupt her. So he kept his gaze steady and stayed silent, encouraging her to go on.

She clenched her hands in her lap. "So, anyway, a woman came in the store today. Louise Armstead. You know her?"

"Yes, I know Louise. She comes in a couple times a week." Fat-free soy latte with extra whip.

"So I was friends with Louise's daughter,

Josie, in high school. Louise told me Josie is moving back here—she's been living and working in Seattle—and that Josie is engaged to be married."

He nodded. Where was this headed?

"Apparently Josie ordered her wedding gown and the bridesmaids' dresses in Seattle, and there was a hitch with the order and the dresses aren't going to be ready in time." Lily took a deep breath. "And I offered to design and make dresses for the whole wedding party."

"That's great," he said, still a bit puzzled about why she was so upset by this.

"Yes, it is. But Josie hasn't agreed she wants me to do it. Yet." Lily shifted on the couch, clearly uneasy. "But if she does, it might pose a problem."

"How so?"

"The wedding's in May and I'm not sure I would have time to design and make the gowns—six of them—and work for you at the same time."

The bottom dropped out of his gut. Oh, man. His shoulders sagged just a bit. Bad news for him. But good news for her. And that was what mattered. So without missing a beat he said, "Hey, that's great! You're a clothing designer.

You should be designing. This is a great opportunity for you."

"Yes, it is," she said. "It would be great to have this in my portfolio. And the experience would be invaluable."

"I agree." It was an incredible opportunity for her. How could he begrudge her that? And it wasn't as if he hadn't known her helping him was only temporary.

"So...you're not mad?" she asked.

No, simply dejected that there was a distinct possibility she wouldn't be there to help out anymore. He'd come to depend on her quiet strength, support and consideration. More than he probably should have. "No, of course not," he said. "How can I be mad when this is clearly something that would be good for your career? You've waited a long time for this opportunity. You should do it, definitely." He had to think of her now, not himself.

Her shoulders visibly relaxed. "Oh, good. I've been really worried about even telling you. I'd feel doubly guilty if you were upset."

"Don't be worried," he said. "You need to do what's best for you."

"What will you do about day care?" she asked, her forehead creasing.

"I'll figure it out," he said, trying to sound confident, even though he wasn't. If Mrs. Jones was out for a very long time—pneumonia could be serious in older people—maybe he'd have to ask Jim to help out after all, though Blake hated to impose with Jim's health up in the air. "Don't give it another thought." Perhaps when Peyton was well Blake could manage her at the store, especially now that he had Jonah on hand.

Lily finally met his gaze. "Thank you so much for understanding."

"Did you think I wouldn't?" He hated the idea that she might have thought the worst of him. Somehow it was important that he was a good man in her eyes.

"Actually, I was pretty sure you'd be happy." She looked at him, straight on, her gorgeous eyes fixed on his. "You're a great guy, Blake. I knew you'd support me in this."

Her statement had his chest going all gooey. He hung his gaze on hers, unable to look away. He felt a pull toward her. She swayed toward him slightly, and all he could think about was kissing her. Holding her in his arms, breathing in her scent. Taking just one moment for what he really wanted.

He slowly bent close and her eyes slid closed as she tipped her head up just a bit—

A baby's cry from the monitor on the coffee table echoed through the room like a gunshot.

He jerked away from Lily, his heart racing. She let out a little squeak, her hand flying up to press her chest, and pulled away quickly.

Peyton. Peyton was crying.

After a shocked moment, he scrambled to his feet just as Lily did the same thing, skittering back a step.

"I'll get her," he said, his voice raspy, surprised he could even form words.

"No," she said, holding out a hand that to his eye was shaking. "Let me get her. I haven't seen her in a while."

He nodded and shoved his hands in his pockets. "All right." Maybe he did need a moment to compose himself. A moment? Ha. A few days was more like it.

Without a word Lily did an about-face and headed out of the room, not quite running, but walking really fast. Getting away. He was careful not to watch her go, keeping his attention on the floor.

When he was alone he rubbed his face, shaking his head. Whew. Talk about a close call. While he couldn't think of anything better than kissing Lily, it was probably for the best Peyton had chosen that exact moment to cry out. Or he would have definitely kissed Lily, and that move, he was sure, while wonderful in the moment, would have been a gigantic mistake in the long run.

He couldn't ignore the truth: he didn't want to risk his heart, and she could be out of their lives as soon as five minutes from now if Josie agreed to the wedding dress designing arrangement.

And even if the wedding design gig didn't work out, Lily would be gone in a few months for sure, on to bigger and better things. To making her dreams come true, as she should. She'd waited a long time for the chance to spread her wings. She deserved this opportunity, and he didn't want to hold her back.

Given all that, he had to do the smart thing here, for him and Peyton, and Lily, too. He had to keep control and keep his distance, let her go whenever necessary and keep in mind that no matter how attracted he was to Lily, no matter how much she impressed him, he couldn't let himself hope for a romance with her.

Even if doing so killed him.

Chapter Ten

As Peyton sat nearby in her bouncy seat, shaking a plastic set of keys, Lily looked at her cell phone for what seemed like the hundredth time. It had been almost twenty-four hours since she'd given her number to Mrs. Armstead, and Lily still hadn't heard from her or Josie. Maybe she never would.

Lily figuratively slapped her head. Why had she even said anything to Blake about any of this? She hadn't planned to, but when she'd arrived last night, she just hadn't been able to keep her mouth shut. She'd just wanted to share her excitement with someone, and Blake had been right there. Now she regretted not being able to keep quiet.

And, significantly, she had wanted to share her news with him. Not Molly. Or Mom. But Blake. Just him. Did that mean anything? Or was she overthinking, making a problem out of nothing?

Her thoughts went back to his reaction to her news, which had warmed her heart through and through, and had only proved to her further what a good person he was. She'd meant it when she'd said he was a great guy with good intentions. He clearly wanted what was best for her, even though it would put him in a bind.

How wonderful was that? He was an unselfish person, no doubt about it.

Unselfish. A bit of guilt niggled at her, setting her conscience on a hard edge. Was she being selfish by even thinking about accepting this job?

Without any thought, she said out loud, "God, am I being selfish? Help me here."

As soon as the words left her mouth, shock rolled through her. She couldn't remember the last time she'd asked the Lord for guidance. Just knowing He was there made her feel so much better. Some of her load lightened, allowing her to focus on reality. She'd sacrificed her life for her family for many years. She had to find her own happiness as a designer, her own place in the world. Or at least try. Lily had to see this through.

She pulled Blake's favorite coffee mug out of the dishwasher, the one that had the words

Anna's Mug, Hands Off emblazoned across the front. All at once, memories of Blake's gaze catching on hers yesterday barreled through her, and Lily put her hand on the counter to steady herself. She would have let him kiss her at that moment. No doubt in her mind. He'd put her own needs ahead of his, and then hit her with those eyes and her guard had almost crumbled at her feet like a wall hit with a wrecking ball.

And at that moment, all she'd wanted was to be in his arms, kissing him, breathing him in.

She shook her head, sighing. Bad. That was bad. Romance wasn't in her plan. It never had been.

But…maybe, if things were different…? What then?

She kicked that thought to the curb. Things were what they were, for good reason. She had a dream, and she couldn't give that up. And she sure didn't want to open herself up to being devastated if she were ever to end up without a man, which, she'd learned through her mom, was a very real possibility for any number of reasons. So there were two very good motivations to put her attraction to Blake on the shelf. Forever.

Needing a distraction, she pulled out her phone and brought up the list of things to do that she kept there, homing in on the items she still had left to do for the Valentine's Day party.

Last night, after she'd left Blake's, she and Molly had made a mad dash to the party store in Pacific City and they'd had a great time picking out decorations. They were all set with that, but Lily still had to put together a list of food items to procure, and she still had to go through Daddy's albums and get them to Grant.

Just then, her cell phone rang in her hand, startling her. She looked at the screen. Josie Armstead.

Lily's tummy bounced as she quickly pressed Answer. "Hello?"

"Lily! Hi, it's Josie." Josie sounded exactly the same—bubbly and effusive. A wave of nostalgia hit Lily.

"Hey, there, you. Long time no talk."

"I know, right? I was so happy when my mom told me she'd seen you."

"It was great to talk to her. Really took me back."

"I'll bet." A pause. "Listen, she told me you offered to design and make all of the dresses for my wedding."

"Yes, I did," Lily said, barely able to say the words while she held her breath.

"Were you serious? Is the offer still open?"

"Yes! It is!" Excitement flitted around inside of Lily like a happy butterfly.

"Well, then, I'd love to have you design the dresses."

"Oh, wow, that's great! I already have some ideas. What's your theme?"

"Rustic chic," Josie said. "You know, burlap, old wood and chalkboards."

"Color scheme?"

"Worn turquoise, along with the mocha and cream neutrals."

"Sounds great." She grabbed a pad of paper. "Why don't you give me your email address and I'll send over some of the ideas I've been thinking of."

"All right." Josie rattled off her email address.

Lily took it down, and then gave Josie hers. "When will you be in town for a face-to-face meeting?"

"The day after tomorrow," Josie said.

"Okay," Lily said, her brain already ticking. "Send me some photos of what you like, and I'll flesh out some rough sketches, and we can go over them when you get here."

"I'll call you the minute we arrive."

"Sounds good." Lily smiled and jumped up and down in place. "I'm really excited about this, Jose," she said, using Josie's childhood nickname.

"Me, too," Josie said. "You are the answer to my prayers."

Floating, Lily said goodbye and hung up. Her first paying fashion design gig. What a milestone. What a relief.

And…it wasn't lost on her that God had heard and answered her own prayer. A sense of wonder filled her, lightening her heart and filling her nearly exhausted well of faith that had been drained since Daddy had died and she'd lost all belief in the power of the Lord.

Welcome back to my life, God. I've missed You.

With that prayer said, she straightened her shoulders and reassured herself she could handle all she'd taken on. She was used to hard work, had seen Mom hold down multiple jobs for a very long time. Lily could do this, wanted to do this. Had to do this for so many reasons.

She bowed her head and sent one more prayer up.

God, please help me to get through this busy, exciting time with grace, patience, and without letting anyone down. And please give me the clearheadedness I'm going to need to deal with the fact that Blake was my go-to person when I had exciting news to share.

* * *

Jonah had to take off early for a family dinner, so Blake did the closing routine by himself. Just as he was about to turn the Open sign in the window to Closed, a forty-something woman he didn't recognize came into the store. She had short platinum-blond hair and wore a stylish black pantsuit. The purse over her shoulder was identical to one Amy had—meaning it was designer and had cost more than he made in a month. That, or it was a very good knockoff.

Either way, she seemed well-to-do.

As she neared the counter, he noted the fine lines around her eyes and what was clearly a very clever makeup job, and he realized she was more than likely older than he'd first thought, probably closer to middle-aged.

A tourist passing through? He was pretty sure she didn't live in town, though it was possible he just hadn't met her.

"May I help you?" he said politely.

She hit him with a dark brown gaze that lacked much warmth. "Are you Blake Stonely?"

Slow but sure, unease snaked up his spine. "Yes, I am." He studied her, but she didn't ring a bell. "Do I know you?"

"No, but you knew my son." Sadness radiated from her eyes. "Rich Van Meter?"

Understanding dawned. Rich was—or had been—Peyton's father. And Anna's fiancé. He'd been killed in Afghanistan shortly after Anna had discovered she was pregnant. "Oh, yes. Mrs. Van Meter." He paused. Wondered what to say, and why she was here. "Um, I'm so sorry for your loss," he said, taking the polite route. If he remembered right, she lived in LA. Rich's funeral had been there. Anna had attended, but Blake hadn't been able to leave town because of the store.

"And I'm sorry for yours," she said. "I was horrified when I heard. Truly horrified."

Ever-present grief rose up in Blake, filling his chest with an ache. "It's been a rough time."

"But you have my granddaughter, a piece of Anna, to help console you, don't you?" Mrs. Van Meter said very, very softly. Too softly, as if she were leading up to something ugly.

"Yes, I do." More trepidation took hold, sending tendrils of suspicion fluttering through Blake.

Mrs. Van Meter's lips wrinkled like a prune, and suddenly she looked old. And mean. And very determined. "And I had no say in that matter, did I?" Her eyes drilled into Blake with the subtlety of a line drive into home run territory. "That just isn't right."

The tendrils of mere suspicion inside of him

turned into razor-sharp daggers of distrust stained with outright fear, and Blake recalled that by Anna's account, Rich's mom hadn't been at all gracious to Anna at the funeral. In fact she'd been downright rude. Anna had attributed Mrs. Van Meter's bad-mannered behavior to grief, and Anna, being the kind soul that she was, had forgiven the woman for her bad conduct. Blake had, too, but now...now he wondered if Anna had been wrong.

Mrs. Van Meter was clearly not here for a social call. She was a piranha on a mission, and Blake had the distinct feeling he was her next meal.

He drew himself up to his full height. "Let's quit beating around the bush and cut to the chase about why you're here," he said, striving to keep his voice well modulated. He had a feeling this woman would take advantage of any weakness, any sign of panic.

She smiled, but it lacked any shred of humor or softness. "Yes, let's," she said, placing her well-manicured hands on the counter. "I'm alone, and all I have left in this world is a job that gives me nice things but bores me to tears." She paused, her eyes hard. Unyielding. "I want more."

Though dread was battering Blake like the waves crashing on the beach just blocks away,

Blake stared her down as if he were made of the hardest granite. Fire with fire. Nothing less to protect Peyton. He steeled himself for what he knew was coming.

"I want my granddaughter, Mr. Stonely," Mrs. Van Meter said, delivering exactly what he'd expected. She pulled an envelope from the purse he knew now was no knockoff. "This is a letter stating my intent to petition for custody of Peyton. My lawyer will be in touch." With that, she slapped the letter down onto the counter, gave him one last razor-sharp, disdainful look and spun around on her heel and marched toward the door.

Despite the panic arcing through Blake like an electric current, he gathered his wits and called out, "Mrs. Van Meter?"

She stopped and turned, her chin at an imperious angle.

He walked out from behind the counter. "Let me be very, very clear," he growled. "Peyton is my niece, and I've been entrusted with her care. While all that is well and good, what matters is that I love that little girl like she's my own daughter." He hit the woman with an icy glare and got so close he could smell her cloying perfume and see the powder that had settled in the wrinkles around her eyes. "You want a battle?"

Her nostrils flared.

He'd take that as a yes. "Then you've got one. I have nothing to lose, you see, as I've already lost it all once before and I can do it again without much fear this time." His finger went up and jabbed the air. "I will not go down without a fight, not with Peyton at stake. Is that clear?"

She blinked, and after a moment, she drew herself up. "Crystal." With a final look of obvious contempt, she took a step back, turned and left the store.

And nothing but the stale smell of her perfume and stark, gut-munching fear was left in her wake.

Blake crumpled the letter in his fist, feeling his power over his world spinning out of his control. Fortunately, Mrs. Van Meter didn't know how much her bid scared him. But he knew all about it, and suddenly it was clear that losing his job had been a mere blip on the screen compared to losing Peyton.

Chapter Eleven

As Lily sat working on sketches for Josie's wedding party attire, Blake walked into the kitchen, home from work.

Concern immediately bolted through Lily. Something was very wrong.

He looked as if he carried the weight of the world on his broad shoulders. His face was drawn, his jaw looked as if it was going to crack and his eyes shined with fatigue. He just had an air about him that screamed something much worse than run-of-the-mill exhaustion.

"What's wrong?"

"What isn't?"

Lily's tummy fell with a *clunk*. "Want to talk about it?"

"Yes, but first, I want to hold my niece." He immediately went over, unhooked Peyton and scooped her up from her high chair. Without missing a beat, he pressed a lingering kiss to her forehead as his eyes slid closed, tenderness evident in every line of his body.

Lily couldn't take her eyes off the man and the baby. Ribbons of tenderness feathered through her, soft yet unmistakable. A lump clogged her throat.

After he hugged Peyton close for a few long moments, he opened his eyes. "She feels cool to the touch."

"Um…" Lily cleared the tightness from her throat. "Yes, the fever is gone." Lily strove to use her usual voice. "The congestion is still hanging around, but it's getting better. I definitely think she's on the mend."

He looked up. "Thank You, Lord."

"Amen," Lily said automatically.

His surprised gaze met hers. "You mean that?"

"Yes, I do. I've realized lately that I've missed having God in my life, thanks to you."

"Glad to hear it," Blake said, nodding. "It's good that you kept an open mind and had a change of heart."

His words warmed her heart and set off butterflies in her midsection. Disconcerted, she picked up the bottle and held it out to him. "Wanna feed her?"

His face softened around the edges a bit.

"Of course." He took the bottle. "Let's go in the living room."

Lily followed him there, and he went over to the couch and sat down, cradling Peyton in his arms, never taking his eyes off her. "Here we go, little girl," he said as he put the bottle in Peyton's mouth.

Lily sat down next to him and tucked her feet up underneath her. "I can tell you've had a rough day, so I want to give you some good news." Excess exhilaration danced through her.

"I could use some of that."

She adjusted herself so she was facing him. "Josie called."

"And?"

"She wants me to design the dresses!" she said, her voice edged in joy.

"Hey, that's great!" he said, his eyes shining with genuine enthusiasm on her behalf. "You've sacrificed so much for your family, and now it's time for you to do your own thing."

His thinking of her needs warmed her heart. "And I was thinking, would you mind if I worked here on the designs while Peyton naps? That way you won't have to find someone else to take care of her."

He nodded as relief gushed through him. "Great idea."

"So you don't mind? I mean, people work from home all the time with kids around. I promise I won't neglect Peyton."

He took her hand in his. "I think it's the perfect solution, and I never had any fears you would neglect her. That isn't you."

She leaned over and hugged him. "Thank you!"

She felt him freeze, his shoulder muscles under her hands tensing.

Mortification spread through her. She'd overstepped. Acted without really thinking. Let her impulses rule. Mistake. She pulled back.

But his free hand stopped her. "Don't go," he said in a husky voice, his eyes locked on hers in a strong grip.

She couldn't for the life of her move a muscle. Or rip her gaze away. Her belly dropped to the floor.

His hand went up and touched her cheek. "You deserve this chance, Lily."

Her heart almost quit beating. "I do?" she whispered, barely capable of speaking, completely enthralled.

He nodded and moved closer. "Yes, you do." His hand moved down to her chin and tilted her face up just a bit. And then he kissed her, his lips soft, his breath fanning out over her.

And it was the most sublime, perfect moment in her life.

She kissed him back, loving the feel of his mouth against hers. She was lost, and never wanted to be found—

Peyton squawked, and reality crashed down on Lily. She dragged herself away, her breath coming fast and furious. "Blake, I can't…"

He dropped his chin. "Oh, man." His head dropped back. "I didn't plan that."

"I know," she replied, scooting back, needing distance. What had she been thinking, getting so close, letting down her guard? Had she lost her sense? Her desire to protect herself? "I shouldn't have, um, hugged you."

"I shouldn't have kissed you," he said, handing her Peyton's empty bottle. "I guess the stress of the day has really gotten to me."

Lily grabbed a burp cloth from the coffee table and handed it to him. Oh, yes, that. His bad day. Head slap. She'd let herself be completely sidetracked from his obvious distress. "What happened?" A change of subject was probably a good idea.

Up Peyton went onto Blake's shoulder. He started patting her back. The muscles in his jaw flexed. "I had a visitor just before closing time."

"Who?"

"Rich's mom," he said tersely.

Lily scrunched her face up. "Rich? Do I know him?"

"Peyton's father."

"Oh." A little barb of apprehension poked her. "What did she want?"

Blake turned an agonized gaze to Lily. "She wants custody of Peyton."

Horror blossomed inside of Lily. *"No."* Little wonder he was distraught. This was terrible news that could shake the foundation of his life.

He nodded. "She's hired a lawyer, and I got the impression she has plenty of money to be able to afford the best."

Lily looked at Peyton lying in his arms. "Well, you have to fight her." Just the thought of him not getting custody made Lily feel ill.

Blake's wretched expression told her he felt as sick about this turn of events as she did. "I know," he replied. "I'm going to."

"I sense a *but*."

He let out a shaky breath. "I just didn't expect someone was going to try to take her away from me." His gaze went to Peyton, who'd dozed off, safe and secure in his arms. "I've only just realized how much I love her," he said so softly Lily could barely hear him.

Hot and burning, tears pushed against Lily's eyelids. "Then you have to fight for her."

"I know. I will fight, with everything in me. Until Jim and Fran, no one fought for me. I won't do that to Peyton."

Lily froze at the clue he'd dropped. Good lead-in to a difficult question. "Is that why you ended up in the foster system?" she asked, keeping her tone soft and even.

"I've never told you about my childhood, have I?" He kept his tone even. Almost too even, as if he were working to stay cool.

She shook her head.

He hesitated. "Let me go put Peyton in her crib and then I'll tell you all about it." He rose, cradling the baby against his broad chest.

"All right." Lily settled back to wait for him, her curiosity about Blake's past exploding. What had happened? Had his parents died? Abandoned him and Anna?

Lily chewed a snag in her fingernail. She couldn't imagine what he must have gone through to land in the system. Losing Daddy had been awful. Blake had somehow lost *both* of his parents at some point. How did someone get over that? Even manage to be the well-adjusted man Blake had turned out to be?

Maybe a person didn't ever really recover from something so devastating.

Blake came back and sat down. "She went right out. Hopefully she's down for the night."

"She does seem to be feeling much better," Lily said, going along with the small talk, giving him time to get his thoughts in line. Or get up his gut for their discussion. Probably both.

Blake sat for a moment, just staring into space. Finally he spoke. "Anna and I grew up in LA. Our dad stuck around until Anna was born—he and our mom never married—and then he robbed a convenience store to support his drug habit and went to prison." Blake shook his head. "We never heard from him again."

Lily's chest caved in. She didn't speak; she simply reached out and put her hand over Blake's.

"Mom was an addict, too, and she never held down a regular job." Blake curled his fingers around Lily's. "She would leave for days at a time and we never knew when she was going to be back."

Horror coagulated inside of Lily. "How—"

"Please let me finish, or I'll never get through this."

She nodded.

"Pretty early on I figured out how to feed us—mostly cereal and peanut butter sandwiches—and we did have a kindly neighbor who brought over food once in a while. But we were essentially alone. Mom would come home, sleep for a couple days and then leave again. We went to school and came home and that was it." He pressed his lips together until they formed a tight line and his grip on Lily's hand was so taut it bordered on painful. "One day when I was fourteen and Anna was eleven the cops showed up and told us Mom had died of a heroin overdose."

Tears gathered in Lily's eyes.

"Jim, my math teacher, had taken me under his wing at school, and he found out about what happened. Within days we were at his and Fran's house, and we never left." Blake sniffed. "They saved our lives. God heard my prayers and found me and Anna a home."

Lily looked at her lap as tears ran down her cheeks.

"My mother and father failed Anna and me our whole lives. They abandoned us, threw us away, didn't ever fight for us." Blake turned. His eyes shone with the trauma of that statement. "That's why I have to fight for Peyton. I never want her to look back at her life and have to come to terms with the fact that her family didn't give a rip about her."

Lily wiped her face with her free hand. "I…I

don't know what to say." Lame, but his story had gutted her completely.

"You don't have to say anything," he said. "In fact, I'd rather you didn't. Talking about that time in my life is hard, and today's been difficult enough as it is."

"No matter the reason, you're doing the right thing, what Anna would have wanted," Lily said.

Blake dragged in a rickety breath and his free hand fisted where it lay on his knee. His face crumbled. "What if I lose Peyton?" he said, his voice cracking. "I...I just can't lose her."

His raw anguish raked across Lily's heart, creating an aching hole. Empathy gushed through her. She knew what it was like to face losing someone you loved. Acting on instinct she leaned in and put her arms around him. A hug of support. Strength. Solidarity. Willingly given in his time of need.

He put his free arm around her, his grip tight. "What am I going to do?"

"We'll figure this out, I promise," she said. "I'm here for you."

And she would be. As a friend. But anything more? She thought back to their kiss. What a mistake that had been. No question. So, right now, anything beyond one friend providing comfort and moral support to another was more than she wanted.

Even with a one-of-a-kind man like Blake.

Blake looked at the crumpled letter from Mrs. Van Meter on his desk and wanted to explode. Her visit had rocked his world, and he was still dealing with the fallout.

Peyton had slept her first good night's sleep in weeks last night, but he sure hadn't. The whole night all he'd been able to think about was Rich's mom walking away with Peyton in her arms.

He'd felt a bit better after he and Peyton had gone to church early this morning. Being close to the Lord always helped him to stay on an even keel. But now, panic spread through him all over again at the thought of losing Peyton. He couldn't let that happen.

But the numbers on the computer spreadsheet in front of him didn't lie. He couldn't afford to pay for a lawyer.

What was he supposed to do? Just let Rich's mom swoop in and take Peyton? No, no way.

He would not abandon her.

Clenching his jaw so hard it hurt, he went over the numbers on the screen in front of him again, hoping maybe he'd missed something, that maybe there was more money somewhere.

But there was nothing more. When he'd moved to town he'd sunk most of what he'd had left into The Cabana, keeping a cushion in savings for unexpected expenses. The store ran on a tight budget every month; by paying himself less and cutting budget corners at home, and by dipping into his cushion fund, he eked out enough to pay Jonah the very minimum legal wage, and to pay Lily. But now, no way did he have enough to pay a healthy retainer to an attorney.

He sagged back in his chair, a dead spot spreading inside of him, at a complete loss.

"Yoo-hoo. Anybody here?"

The door to his office opened.

Lily stood on the other side, pushing Peyton's stroller, wearing an unusual black-and-brown jacket that had to be custom made by her. Peyton sat in the stroller, looking as cute as a button with her pink fleece coat and knit hat. She waved her arms when she saw him.

What a sight for sore eyes. And worried heart.

He stood. "Hey, there, you two. To what do I owe this pleasure?"

Lily came around the stroller and pulled Peyton's hat off. "I had a bit of a rough morning, so when this little gal woke up, I thought we should just motor on down here and pay you a visit."

He frowned. "Rough morning? With Peyton?"

"Well, the truth is, she did spit cereal all over the place so I had to bathe her and clean up. But I'm also having major design block, and the material Josie wants for her dresses is special order and I won't be able to get it in time so I need to come up with an alternative."

"Oh, wow. You've got a lot of plates in the air."

"Yes, I do. But I managed to settle Peyton, and I've got a line on some material I think Josie will like, so I figured after all that problem solving, I deserved a walk and some fresh air."

"You're a superwoman."

"Not nearly, but I do feel pretty good about being able to multitask."

"You should be proud," he said, liking how she'd worked through her mini crisis.

"Let's just say I need a break, too. How did you know?"

"I'm good that way," Lily said with a quirk of her lips.

"Yes, you are." Uncannily she always seemed to know how to brighten his day. "How's my little girl?" He bent and picked up

Peyton, holding her against his shoulder. He pressed his nose to her bald head, loving the smell of fresh baby shampoo mixed with the scent of fresh air.

Lily's eyes fell on the stack of flyers he'd printed earlier on the edge of the desk. "Hey." She picked one up. "These turned out great!"

"Yes, they did, thanks to one very talented designer who took pity on me."

"You just needed a little push in the right direction."

"Yeah, right." Suddenly the walls of his office seemed to collapse on him. "You up for a little more walking?" He rubbed his gritty eyes. "I need to get out of here."

Lily frowned, and then she noticed his open laptop. "What's got you so stressed?"

He put the baby back in her stroller and grabbed his coat from the hook on the back of the door. "I'll tell you outside." Maybe Lily could help him figure out what to do. She was levelheaded, smart and had a way of making his problems seem manageable.

"Lead the way, then," she said, slipping Peyton's hat back on her head. "Maybe we can go get some sundaes at I Scream for Ice Cream."

"Good idea," he said. He couldn't remember the last time he'd gone out for a treat in the middle of the day. Some fresh air, a hot fudge sundae and some time with Lily and Peyton were just what he needed.

Soon enough he'd be back pounding his head against the computer. The depressing numbers weren't going anywhere. Unfortunately.

He left Jonah in charge and soon Blake, Lily and Peyton were on the wooden boardwalk lining Main Street. He pushed the stroller and Lily walked close beside him.

The sky was clear and the sun was shining. A stiff breeze blew, but it was a gorgeous day for February.

They walked in silence for a block or so, admiring the primroses the Main Street business owners had planted in pots in front of their stores.

Halfway to the ice cream parlor, Lily faced him, her gaze probing. "What's going on? You seem upset."

"Yeah, you could say that." Suddenly cold, he fastened the top button on his coat. "I was going over spreadsheets."

"Okay."

"And they don't tell a pretty story."

"How so?"

He hesitated. Could he really admit to Lily that he was essentially broke? That he was on the brink of failing again? He shuddered inside.

Turning, he saw her looking up at him, appearing steady and calm. He needed steady and calm. And that was Lily.

He cleared his throat. "Um, well, the thing is, I, uh…"

Stopping, she pulled on his sleeve. "Blake."

"Yes?"

"Just spit it out, okay? You should know by now I won't judge."

Yes, he knew that. It was one of the things he liked most about her. "Right." He gripped the stroller handle so hard his fingers ached. "The thing is, I don't have the money to pay for a lawyer to fight for custody."

To her credit, she didn't react negatively. Good on her. "Ah, I see." She chewed on her lip. "Well, let's talk solutions."

"I like how you skipped the details and jumped right to the problem-solving stage."

"Makes the most sense to me. No reason to discuss the nitty-gritty." She pulled Peyton's blanket up higher. "Besides, the whys don't matter, do they?"

"No, I guess not." Truthfully, he was relieved not to have to dissect his financial situation. Admitting outright to another failure would be difficult. He had a sneaking suspicion Lily knew that, that she was helping him save face. Bless her for keeping his feelings in mind.

"So, what are your options?"

"Few." That single word just about killed him.

"Such as?"

"Jim might loan me the money," Blake said. "But I really don't want to go that route. He and Fran have had a lot of medical expenses, and I feel like they've already done enough for me."

"Okay, so that's out. What else have you got?"

His hands tightened on the stroller handle. "There's only one other option."

Lily stopped at the door to I Scream for Ice Cream. "What's that?"

"I could sell The Cabana," he said, the words bitter on his tongue.

Lily's jaw fell. "You're kidding."

"Wish I was."

"Okay, wow." She moved out of the doorway. "That seems a bit drastic."

"Drastic times, drastic measures."

"Good point."

He went on. "I could borrow against the business, but honestly, with business so bad, I'm sure I wouldn't get approved for a loan."

Lily was silent for a few seconds, and it

looked as if the wheels were turning in her mind. "I wish I could help somehow."

"I have to figure this out on my own." A stream of sadness filtered through him. Sometimes being alone wasn't fun.

Peyton started to fuss, reminding him he wasn't completely alone. As they entered the ice cream shop, he glanced over at Lily, thinking of the impact she'd had on his life in such a short amount of time. Standing next to her at the counter, doing something as ordinary as ordering ice cream, he couldn't help but see a glimpse of what his life could be like with her: taking walks, getting treats, just talking. And her always there for him...

He watched Lily lovingly tend to Peyton and wondered if he wanted something more in his life, something lasting. Someone by his side. Someone like Lily?

No. He couldn't let his hopes go to a forbidden place, a place where he would put himself in a position to be left hurting and alone in the end. Anything between him and Lily was just a crazy dream. Good thing dreams didn't cost a thing. As long as they were managed right, of course.

Once they had their sundaes in hand, they situated themselves at one of the small round tables the owner of the store, Phoebe Winters, had set up for customers. He pulled Peyton from the stroller and settled her on his lap. His mouth watering, he picked up his sundae to dig in.

Peyton's eyes followed his spoon and she let out a loud whine and kicked her legs and waved her arms.

"She wants some," Blake said, grinning.

"Of course she does," Lily replied. "It's ice cream."

"Can she have it?"

"Sure. She's had milk in her cereal." Lily gave him a sideways glance. "But be prepared to share from now on."

"Okay, sweet pea, here you go." He scooped up a tiny amount of ice cream and held it close to Peyton's mouth, steadying her so she could take a taste. She squealed in delight and his heart lightened a bit.

He alternated between eating his ice cream and feeding Peyton bites. Through the window at the front of the store, wispy clouds floated in the sky like ribbons of fluff.

He'd needed this sojourn. For a moment all of his cares moved to the background.

After a companionable silence, Lily finished her sundae and pulled out napkins she'd stashed in her pocket. "Let's get you cleaned up," she said, gently wiping Peyton's ice-cream-stained lips and cheeks.

He surreptitiously studied Lily, noting that her eyes right now were the color of dark emeralds and that she had just the barest dusting of freckles on her nose. She'd corralled her hair back with something, and he couldn't help but notice the perfect lines of her smooth cheeks and lips.

A sense of contentment settled down around him, warm and solid, and he suddenly wished he could freeze his life in this moment.

Lily's gaze caught on him. "What are you thinking?"

He adjusted Peyton on his lap. "I was just wishing I could freeze this moment." He felt too happy to brush off her question.

"It has to be the ice cream," she said. "Comfort food for me."

He suspected his present happiness had nothing to do with ice cream and everything to do with her, but that thought spoken aloud would probably freak her—and him—out. So instead he said, "That must be it."

She turned so she was facing him. "So, let's talk about you selling The Cabana. How are you feeling about that?"

His mood took a downward turn. "Terrible." But she didn't know the whole reason why. Maybe it was time for him to share that part of his past with her. After all she'd done for him, he owed her the truth. "I…um, had a pretty big job failure in New York, and I swore that I'd succeed here no matter what."

She frowned. "So you view selling The Cabana as a failure?"

"Yeah, I do." He watched a seagull land on a car parked on Main Street and then dive-bomb at something on the sidewalk. Probably some bit of food someone had dropped.

"Well, you shouldn't," she said. "You're selling it for Peyton, right?"

"Right."

"So how can that ever be seen as a failure?"

Something heavy lifted from his shoulders. "I never thought of it that way."

"Well, you should. You're being unselfish, and sacrificing something important for Anna's daughter. You should look at this as a good thing, Blake." Lily smiled. "A very good thing."

His mood lifted even higher. "Thank you for your perspective. I really appreciate it."

"Anytime," she said, her mouth curving into a shy smile.

He knew she was there for him. Not for forever, though. Come June, she wouldn't be around to help him see the positive side of things. Once again he thought about how much he was going to miss her when she was gone. But there was nothing he could do about that except take a page from her book and stay the course and try to see the bright side of things, even though one of his biggest cheerleaders would be long gone, making her own dreams finally come true.

She deserved that, and he would do everything possible to make sure she followed through on her plans, but he suspected his sorrow to see her leave would never really go away or diminish. Not even after she was the darling of the LA fashion community.

And he would be her biggest fan. Even if from afar.

Chapter Twelve

Jim handed a two-by-four to Blake. "That one goes over there," he said, pointing to the far side of the area in which Blake was helping him build a new back deck. "These, too." Jim pointed to the pile of planks to his left.

"Gotcha." Blake bent and picked up three or four pieces of wood and took them over and set them in the designated area.

As he rose, he wiped his forearm over his brow. It was a rare and relatively warm and sunny February day in Moonlight Cove, and he and Jim had decided they'd better get the deck framed while they could do so in dry weather rather than pouring rain, which was more typical for this time of year.

Besides, replacing Jim and Fran's rotting deck had been in the queue for a while. Now that Jim was feeling better, and had been told his biopsy had come back benign, it was time to make a new deck happen.

And there was nothing like physical labor to distract Blake from the custody situation simmering like a pot about to boil over.

Fran stuck her head out of the sliding door. "The baby is down for her nap. I'm going to start lunch. Is grilled cheese okay?"

"Fine," Blake said at the same time Jim did.

"Okay. It'll be ready in about ten minutes." Fran slid the door closed.

Jim took a drink of water from the sports bottle he'd put on the sawhorse. "So Fran tells me Mrs. Jones is coming back tomorrow?"

Blake took a swig from his own bottle. "Yep, she's fully recovered and raring to go." The day care situation would go back to normal, and he wouldn't be seeing Lily every day anymore. He'd been trying not to let that bring him down, but there was no denying he'd really liked having Lily around. His life was going to seem very empty without her, though he was trying not to dwell on that sad reality. He'd known this day was coming since he'd met Lily. He'd deal as best he could.

"How long was she out?"

"Two weeks," Blake said.

"Wow, that long?" Jim shook his head and picked up a hammer. "Time sure flies."

"Yep, it sure does. Sometimes that's a good thing. Sometimes not." Blake grimaced. "Like when a custody battle is looming."

"Where are you with the custody thing?" Jim asked.

Blake's gut clenched. "Things are moving forward now. My lawyer has heard from Mrs. Van Meter's lawyer and they're doing their lawyer thing. The initial hearing is scheduled for the end of next week." Blake held back telling Jim about his plans to sell the store; telling everybody would just make his decision more real, and that was a tough one to handle.

Jim turned and studied Blake. "What aren't you telling me?"

"You know me too well."

"Yeah, I do." Jim pushed his sunglasses up onto his head. "Now spill."

Time to tell the story. "I had some trouble coming up with the money for the lawyer."

"Why didn't you tell me? We could have helped out."

"I told you, you've already done enough."

Jim waved a hand in the air. "You know what I think about that, but it's your call."

Blake simply nodded.

"So I take it you got the money somewhere?"

"Uh-huh." Blake grabbed a few more boards.

After several long seconds, Jim said, "Mind if I ask where?"

The boards fell into the pile with a clatter. "I was waiting until I had the details in place to say anything, and it looks like it's all a go."

"What's all a go?"

"I'm selling the store," Blake blurted before he could think better of it. Oh, well. Jim would know eventually.

Jim hit Blake with a sobering gaze. "Tell me you're joking."

"No joke." Blake grabbed his tool belt and hooked it around his hips. "I needed the cash, and one of the regulars at the store knew someone who was interested in buying The Cabana and turning it into a Java Joint."

"The Oregon company that's expanding into Washington?"

"Yep. They have twenty very successful stores in Oregon, and a familiar name behind them, and they're anxious to close the deal. I sign the paperwork next week." He did his best to sound matter-of-fact, but inside he was crumbling. He could only hope he'd eventually come to terms with losing the business. His only consolation was that Peyton was worth any price and that as Lily had said, the bitter sense of failure that came from losing

The Cabana would be outweighed by keeping custody of Peyton.

He prayed he came out on the winning end of the custody fight.

"You put your heart and soul into that place," Jim said, his face pinched. "I hate to see you have to sell it."

"I hate to do it, too. But I'll do whatever necessary to protect that little girl."

Jim pressed a hand to Blake's shoulder. "You sure about this?"

"Dead sure." Through many sleepless nights and fevered prayers since Rich's mom had handed him that letter, Blake had run in circles trying to solve this problem. He was convinced this was the only way. So be it. "In fact, Lily helped me realize that this isn't a failure and helped me come to terms with losing the store."

"Ah, Lily," Jim said with a lift of his brow. "She's sure helped you a lot lately."

"Yes, she has." Hoping to deter Jim from the subject of Lily, Blake bent and rummaged through the toolbox at his feet. "Where's your level? We're gonna need that."

"I must have left it in the garage," Jim said, and then went silent.

After a few beats of quiet, Blake straightened and turned.

Jim stood there, staring at him intently.

"What?" Though Blake was pretty sure he knew what was going through Jim's mind, and it had everything to do with how Blake felt about Lily.

"Let's talk about Lily."

Bingo. "I'd rather talk about you getting that level while I start marking where the cross supports are going to go."

"I'm sure you would, but I think we need to talk about you and Lily."

"There is no me and Lily," Blake said. "She's done with taking care of Peyton, and she's leaving for LA in a few months and isn't planning on coming back. End of story."

"Would you like a different ending to that story?"

"What I want doesn't matter."

"Since when?" Jim asked.

"Since I decided that."

"Why did you decide that?"

"Because that's what Lily wants, okay?" Blake swiped his arm over his forehead. "She wants to go do this reality show in LA. She's waited forever to do it. I'm not going to stand in her way."

"I'm asking you what you want," Jim persisted.

"You're not going to let this go, are you?"

"Nope."

Jim was one of the most stubborn people Blake knew. Maybe he did need to talk about Lily. He'd certainly been thinking about her a lot lately. "I don't know what I want." Blake shook his head. "All I know is I'm going to miss her, Peyton's going to miss her, and if things were different..." He trailed off, hating that he'd even gone the wishy-washy hopeful route. He usually tried to be more sensible than that.

"Maybe they *can* be different," Jim said. "Have you talked to her about how you feel?"

Blake's stomach lurched. "No, I haven't, and I'm not going to." Just the thought of hashing out his feelings with Lily made him sweat. "She doesn't need someone holding her back and I'm not ready to set myself up to get hurt."

"Well, whatever story you want to tell yourself," Jim said, shrugging.

"What do you mean by that?"

"Well, the way I see it, as long as you hang yourself on the I'm-being-thoughtful-of-Lily hook, you're safe."

A chill spread through Blake. "You think that's what I'm doing?" He shoved out the words. But he already knew the answer to that question.

"Yep. And little wonder, what with your

history. You're wary of love. I get that." Jim canted his head. "But there has to be a balance, you see, between not wanting to take a risk and losing something wonderful."

Blake mulled that over, trying to take it all in without freaking out.

"In other words," Jim went on, "you might keep your heart safe by telling yourself a story, but in the end you get hurt anyway."

"By losing Lily."

"Exactly," Jim said, pointing a finger at Blake. "Are you prepared for that?"

Something cracked inside of Blake and he winced. He would lose Lily if he held all of this in, and she'd go to LA as planned and he'd stay here. "I'm not sure I'm ready to take the chance," he said.

"Your call," Jim said. "Just wanted to be sure you had all of the angles covered." He picked up a hammer. "What are you going to do for work after you sell the store?"

Blake was grateful for the topic change. "The guy from Java Joint has asked me to run the place."

"Well, that's some consolation."

"Actually, I'm trying to look at it like this— I get to work at the store without any of the headaches of owning it."

"Good strategy," Jim said. "But if I know you, it won't be the same as being in charge."

"No, it won't. But I'm doing my best to look at the bright side." Lily would, wouldn't she?

"Just as Anna always did."

Her, too. "Yes, like Anna." He couldn't go wrong if he emulated those two great women.

With a furrowed brow, Jim considered Blake. "She would be proud of you, and I am, too."

Blake's eyes burned.

Jim stood still for a moment and then quickly flipped his sunglasses back into place. A moment later, he swiped a finger under the bottom rim of the glasses. "Stupid allergies." He sniffed. "Pollen count must be up."

Blake dropped his head and wiped his own eyes on the cuff of his long-sleeved T-shirt. "You were reading my mind."

A stiff breeze, straight off the ocean, blew through, rattling the leafless trees. Blake settled his baseball cap more firmly on his head and looked up. Clouds the color of stone loomed to the far west and the telltale scent of coming rain hovered in the air. "Looks like it's going to rain soon."

"Figures," Jim said. "Guess we'd better stop shooting the breeze and get to work."

"Guess we'd better," Blake replied, glad he

had something to take his mind off what Jim had said about Lily.

But Blake knew well and good that the reprieve from his worries was only temporary and that sooner or later he was going to have to deal with his complicated feelings for Lily.

And then he'd have no choice but to face head-on the inevitable fallout.

Lily straightened a pan of cookie dough brownies on the church banquet table, then stepped back to review her handiwork. She'd stayed up half the night making them. The other half she'd dedicated to working on the designs for Josie's wedding in preparation for the meeting she'd had with the bride-to-be earlier today.

Honestly, at around 1:00 a.m. last night, Lily had had her doubts that she could get everything done for the dance and Josie. But she'd stayed focused and had prioritized all of her tasks, and voilà, everything had been accomplished.

Yes, she was tired. Bone tired. But the sense of self-accomplishment she'd felt all day far outweighed her exhaustion. She was still standing, albeit wearily.

She had done it all. Thankfully Mrs. Jones

was coming back to work tomorrow, and Lily would have a lot more time to devote to her bridal design work.

Though she would miss Blake and Peyton.

Yanking herself from that dangerous train of thought, she looked around, smiling at the oodles of hearts of every size and shape and enough red, white and pink crepe paper to string around the church four times that she and Molly had spent an hour putting up earlier today after church services. A punch bowl filled with pink lemonade and heart-shaped ice cubes sat nearby.

There were already quite a few people here—what seemed like an equal mix of guys and gals—and '80s dance music played from the sound system Grant had set up in the corner. He was also serving as an impromptu deejay.

Molly caught Lily's eye and came over. "Everything looks great," she said.

"Yes, it does." She high-fived Molly. "We make a good team."

"Is Blake coming?" Molly asked without preamble.

Lily froze. "Why do you ask?"

"Just curious."

"I don't think so," Lily responded. Though a

part of her wished he would come. A part she was trying to ignore.

"Did you invite him?"

"No!" Lily immediately said.

"Whoa. You're a bit touchy." Molly scrutinized her. "Why is that?"

Lily sighed. Molly wasn't going to let this go. So be it. Maybe Lily needed to talk. "Part of me really wishes he would come."

"What's wrong with that?"

"I don't want to wish for anything that has to do with Blake."

"Sometimes what we want is beyond our control."

"I'm discovering that."

"Often our emotions are trying to tell us something. And sometimes we need to listen to them."

A trill of alarm rang in Lily. "What if it's something we don't want to hear?"

"Well, I guess you can ignore what your inner voice is trying to tell you."

"I like that plan," Lily said, nodding, wishing it were that cut-and-dried, but knowing it wasn't. Too bad.

"I liked it, too, once upon a time," Molly replied solemnly. "But in the end, listening to our innermost thoughts is smarter than ignoring what they're saying and regretting it in the end."

"How can I regret doing what I've always wanted?"

"Maybe what you've always wanted isn't what it's cracked up to be if you're all alone and missing an important piece of your life." Molly gave her a blunt stare. "And has it occurred to you that maybe what your heart and brain want aren't necessarily mutually exclusive?"

Shock spread through Lily. "Funny you would say that. I had that very thought a few minutes ago." What did that all mean?

Before Molly could reply, Lily's eye caught on the door. And on the man who'd just arrived at the party looking yummy in a pair of dark jeans and a blue button-down shirt.

With her tummy cartwheeling, she grabbed Molly's arm. "Blake's here!"

Molly turned. "I guess he is." She nodded slowly.

"What should I do?" Lily asked, panic eating away at the edges of her composure.

"Well, maybe this is your opportunity to listen to your gut and see where it takes you."

Trepidation rolled through Lily. "I don't think I can."

"Sure you can." Molly rose and grabbed

Lily's hand. "Just spend some grown-up time with him and keep an open mind."

"I'm scared." Of getting hurt. Of being dependent on Blake. Of ending up with a broken heart like Mom.

"Risk is scary. But it's also necessary sometimes," Molly said. "You need to know what's going on between you and Blake before you can truly move on with your life."

A chilling sense of inevitability flushed through Lily. *God's plan?* "Maybe you're right. Maybe I need to know." Lily sucked in a breath and let it out slowly.

Molly gave her a little push toward Blake. "Yes, you do."

Lily made her way to the handsome man by the dessert table, feeling as if her world could tilt the wrong way tonight. Or the right way. She clenched her hands at her sides, hating the not knowing, the uncertainty.

She drew near Blake, her legs trembling and her heart thumping louder than the bass from the music playing. And though she knew she had to face this dilemma down once and for all in order to be able to move ahead, she was more terrified than she'd ever been in her life.

And for the first time in what seemed like forever, she was glad she had God to lean on. She had a feeling she was going to need Him.

Chapter Thirteen

Blake's breathing went haywire when he saw Lily coming toward him. She looked really great dressed in a pair of form-fitting narrow-legged jeans and a flowy pink top that skimmed her hips. She had her hair pulled up on her head and a few tendrils hung down around her pale cheeks.

And…she looked scared to pieces, as if she were approaching a lion in its den. He frowned. She stopped dead in her tracks. He instantly smiled big and motioned her forward.

"Hey," he said when she reached his side.

She cleared her throat. "Um, hey."

He'd never seen her look more awkward. "You look…nervous."

"Well, you said you weren't coming, so I, um, didn't expect to see you here."

He wasn't sure why that would throw her,

but decided to let it go. "Yeah, I know, I wasn't planning on coming. But then after Jim and I finished his deck and Fran offered to keep Peyton, I figured I might as well take advantage of a babysitter and come here for a while." In all truth, he'd decided to come mostly because he'd wanted to see Lily. Saying goodbye was proving to be harder than he'd thought it would be. Way harder.

He was still trying to get his brain around what that meant. Though he wasn't sure he was going to like what he discovered.

"Well, good." She smiled woodenly. "Glad you could make it."

He studied her for a moment, noting her stiff posture and rigid jaw. She looked like a statue of Lily, a mere copy with the life sucked out. This wasn't her. "Sorry to mention this again, but you're acting weird." He hooked his hands in his back pockets. "What's going on?"

She shifted, her lips rolled in. "The thing is—"

Before she could say more, the song "Footloose" started blaring.

"I love this song," she yelled, her face wreathed in a sudden smile. Suddenly she looked like her regular self.

"Me, too," he hollered back. He should ask

her to dance, but suddenly he was as tongue-
tied as a middle schooler at his first dance.

As he stood next to her, wrestling with his
own fears, everyone on the sidelines made
their way to the dance floor in the middle of
the basement. In a few short moments, he and
Lily were the lone holdouts.

He felt like an idiot. A gutless idiot. Ri-
diculous. He knew Lily well now. No reason
he shouldn't ask her to participate, right? He
sucked in a large breath, then looked at Lily
and held out his hand. "You wanna dance?"

She paused for a millisecond, her eyes wide,
and then she placed her hand in his. "Let's go!"

Nodding in time to the '80s beat, he led her
to the edge of the floor, loving the feeling of
her hand in his. As he arrived in the spot he'd
chosen, a sudden awkwardness engulfed him.
He'd never been a great dancer. In fact, Amy
had told him he had terrible rhythm. Second
thoughts burned through him, and he was suddenly sure he was going to make a huge fool of
himself. In front of Lily, the only woman he'd
wanted to impress in a long, long time. His
cheeks warmed and his legs turned to steel.
No way was he going to be able to even walk
like this, much less dance.

He turned to her to beg off, maybe, but she

was already dancing, kicking up her feet and throwing her arms around.

She gave him a goofy grin. "Dance!" she shouted, boogying around in a circle, her feet doing some crazy thing as she rolled her wrists one over the other like a disco girl on fire.

Her teasing smile and upbeat, unembarrassed attitude were contagious. His reservations dissipated and his shoulders relaxed. The beat rolled through him and his feet started moving in time. His legs loosened up, and though he was still self-conscious, he managed to get into the groove a bit.

The beat was infectious, and soon he was letting his hips swing a little and his arms move, never taking his eyes off Lily, who proved herself to be a regular dancing queen.

Her carefree dance style had him chuckling, and loosening up even more. Happiness wove through him, casting out all of the worry and stress that he'd been dealing with lately.

Toward the end of the song, someone started a conga line, which snaked around the outside of the dance floor.

Lily crooked a hand. "Come on!" She ran to the end of the line and grabbed on to Molly's shoulders.

Blake hustled on over and got in back of Lily and carefully placed his hands on her slim shoulders and followed the line around, step, step, step, kick and so on. Lily laughed and looked back at him, her eyes glowing with unmistakable delight. More joy bubbled up inside of him and he found himself grinning and laughing as he danced around like a kid, holding tight to Lily, more relaxed and carefree than he'd been in years.

Too soon the song came to an end, and the conga stopped. Claps went up, and he joined in.

Lily turned, but before she said anything, the music segued into a synthesizer sound unique to a slow song by Foreigner, one of his favorite bands. Some people left the dance floor, but most stayed and started swaying in time with the song as they danced close.

He froze, unsure—did they dance, walk off the floor, what? Would Lily want to slow dance with him? The last thing he wanted to do was make her uncomfortable.

Just as the singing started—a guy saying he'd been waiting for a girl like the one right in front of him—Lily backed away, her eyes down.

Suddenly Blake knew that he didn't want to let her go right now. It was just one dance, one time for him to act in the here and now. He wanted to dance with her in his arms.

Without overanalyzing his motives, he grabbed her hand. "I love this song," he said.

Her eyes went big, and he saw the indecision warring inside of her. He stared at her steadily, his gaze homing in on hers, willing her to accept. To let go for once.

Pulling her gaze away, she looked down, her fingers clutching the hem of her swirly top.

His hopes crashed and burned, and just when he thought she was going to refuse, her gaze rose and met his. She nodded and said, "All right."

As the chorus rolled around and the meat of the song made an appearance, she stepped near, her eyes locked on his. Barely able to breathe, he took her in his arms, holding her close, but not too close; again, he didn't want to make her uncomfortable or regret dancing with him. Never that.

Her feelings were important.

Her arms went around his waist, and he was sure he felt her hands tremble there. His were shaking, too, and it was all he could do to swing slightly side to side in time to the swelling music. After a few bars, though, he had settled in and was in perfect tune with her steps, moving as one.

He rested his chin next to her head, breathing in the fresh scent of her shampoo, wondering if he'd ever experienced a more perfect moment in time.

As the singer delivered the message of the song and Blake danced with Lily, her heart pressed against him, he suddenly knew the lyrics expressed how he felt. He had been waiting for a girl like her. And now, here she was, in his arms, making his heart feel whole and brave and wanting so much more.

Wanting her forever.

The song ended too soon. When the last note rang out, Lily pulled back out of his grip and her eyes met his. He wasn't sure what he saw there, but it seemed to be a combination of fear and regret. His gut pitched. He hated that he'd stirred those emotions in her. Especially since he was feeling exactly the opposite.

He thrust out a hand. "Lily…"

She stepped back, out of his reach, her posture poised to flee.

His hand fell to his side. "Let's talk."

"No," she said, shaking her head. "I, um…I can't. I have to run an errand I forgot about."

Desperation cut a jagged line through him. "Don't run away," he implored. "The party's just begun."

"I have to go," she said. "I…just have to."

He'd clearly spooked her. And that wasn't what he'd intended. But what could he do? It wasn't as if he could tie her up and force her to stay. "Okay," he said. "I'll call you in the morning." Mrs. Jones would be there bright and early, so he wouldn't be seeing Lily then.

A pall descended over him, obliterating his happiness in a thick, gray fog.

"I'll call you," she said, already moving away. Running away. From him.

He wanted to beg her not to forget to call, but that would sound pathetic and put more pressure on her. So he simply said, "All right."

She lifted a hand. "Bye."

"Bye," he replied.

He kept his eyes on her, watched her stop and talk to Molly, who seemed to be trying to talk Lily out of leaving. Blake held his breath, hoping Molly would convince her to stay. But Lily shook her head, said something, hugged Molly and then grabbed her coat from a chair and hustled out the door without a look back.

Blake stood alone in the middle of the dance floor, his head down, missing Lily already. One thought gouged him hard from the inside out.

How was he ever going to let an amazing woman like Lily walk out of his life for good?

Lily arrived home from the Valentine's Day dance, her thoughts awhirl with full-fledged panic. She rolled the car windows down and breathed in the fresh, cold air, trying to calm down, stay grounded. But achieving her composure right now, with that dance with Blake swirling in her mind, was useless.

She'd almost quit breathing when he'd asked her to dance when the slow Foreigner song had come on. For a long moment, she was going to refuse, determined to keep up her wall. But the need to be close to him overrode her wish to keep him at a distance, and she'd said yes, hoping she could take the feel of being in his arms and be happy with just that and no more.

The second she'd stepped into his arms, she'd felt as if she was exactly where she was supposed to be. Safe. Warm. Contented. As if she'd found what she'd been waiting for, echoing the lyrics of the song in a profound way that was impossible to ignore.

Having his arms around her had been blissful. Wonderful. She hadn't wanted the song to stop. Would have been happy to dance in his arms all night long.

Too soon, the song ended and she'd stepped out of his arms, her thoughts chaotic as she wished another slow song would come along and they could do the whole thing over again.

Reality had hit her then like a rocket blast: she was in big trouble, and the brief taste of delight and rightness she'd had would never be enough unless she cut herself off right now.

For someone who had very valid reasons for wanting to avoid love she'd been much too captivated by Blake. Full of doubts, fear and confusion, she'd panicked, made an excuse and left then and there, with the devastating truth reverberating in her brain.

She was so close to falling in love with Blake she could barely see where *like* ended and *love* began.

No, no, no.

How had she let this happen? She'd made up her mind to keep Blake in the employer/ friend/Peyton's daddy compartment, to stay focused on her future as a designer and all that entailed, to make sure she never experienced her mom's heartbreak. But she'd failed miserably. Apparently her heart had a mind of its own, and it was taking over her brain at the moment.

What was she going to do now?

Pray. She had to pray. She bowed her head and entreated God to guide her, help her to know what to do that would stay true to herself and her dreams, but also stay true to her heart.

Just as that prayer went up to Him, her cell phone rang. She grabbed it from her purse, noting that the phone's screen said the "Unknown" caller was calling from California. Hmm. She didn't recognize the number.

Shrugging, she pressed Answer. "Hello?" she said tentatively.

"Hello. May I please speak to Lily Rogers?"

"This is Lily."

"Oh, good." A pause. "My name is Daniel Esperanza, and I'm a producer for the show *Project Fashion.*"

Lily's heart did a jig and her jaw went slack. *What!* "Oh, um, hi," she somehow managed to say, though she was pretty sure she sounded like a complete dork.

"I'm calling because we've had someone drop out of the current competition at the last moment. We found your online application and were quite impressed by your portfolio. We'd like to ask you to fill that spot."

Lily couldn't believe what she'd just heard. "Oh, wow."

"Would you be interested?"

"Yes, yes, of course," she replied, shaking so hard she almost dropped her phone. No way could she say no. She'd been waiting for this moment for years. Had dreamed about it more times than she could count.

"We're starting to film the upcoming season next week, and all of the contestants are arriving Wednesday. How does that timeline work for you?"

Shock rolled through her. In three days? That fast? She gripped her cell so hard her fingers hurt. She'd have to design Josie's dresses remotely, but she'd make that work somehow. She'd learned that she could successfully juggle multiple tasks. "That would be fine." More than fine. It was wonderful. Perfect. A dream come true. An answer to a prayer. Then it hit her—she didn't have enough money saved yet. Her hopes crashed to earth.

Daniel went on. "Since it's such short notice, we'd be willing to pay all of your expenses to get down here, and you'll get a daily stipend for living expenses, too. We can book a flight for you and email you the e-ticket."

Her hopes soared again. "That would be great," she said, barely able to contain her excitement. The airfare was a big chunk of her anticipated expenses. If she were careful, and she got a stipend, she'd be able to stretch the money she had to last long enough, especially since she'd made extra working for Blake.

"Excellent." The sound of rustling paper carried over the phone line. "I'd like to send all of the details and paperwork via email. Is the email address you listed on your application still current?"

"Yes, yes, it is," she said breathlessly.

"Great. I'll send that as soon as we end this call. All of our contact information will be detailed in that email."

"O-okay," she said, a bit dazed by the turn of events. But beyond thrilled, too.

"Gina Mathers from our travel department will call you in the morning to finalize flight information. Can she call you on this number?"

"Yes, this number is great."

"Our legal department will also be contacting you. Same number, I presume?"

"Yes."

"Okay, then. I'll send the email. You can read it and send back the pertinent items, which will be noted in the email, via overnight delivery tomorrow. Once you get travel and legal details squared away, we'll be all set."

"Okay, sounds perfect," she said, happiness and excitement going wild inside of her. *Finally.*

"We're looking forward to welcoming you to the *Project Fashion* family."

"I'm looking forward to that, too," she said in all truthfulness. She'd been anticipating this moment for years. Her heart pirouetted.

"Be sure and call if you have any questions, all right?"

"All right."

"Goodbye."

"Bye." With trembling hands, she pressed End Call and sat back in the driver's seat, unable to believe what had just happened. She was going to LA. In just a day or two.

"Woo-hoo!" Nervous anticipation, along with a huge dose of out-and-out exhilaration, flashed through her. Yes, yes, yes! Finally her dream was coming true. And even sooner than she'd thought—

Her elation crashed to the ground. She'd promised Blake she'd attend the first custody hearing with him, though he didn't know when, exactly, that would be.

How could she let him down?

She squared her jaw. Somehow, someway, she'd come back for the hearing, even if she had to max out her credit card to do so.

A vision of Blake and Peyton rose in Lily's mind. Some of her excitement dissipated, only to be replaced by a hard, cold lump of regret. It would be hard to leave them behind, yes. But she *had* to take this once-in-a-lifetime opportunity. Everything she'd ever wanted was right in front of her, there for the taking. She couldn't stay in Moonlight Cove, and she'd always known that.

This was what she was supposed to do.

Unbidden, memories of dancing with Blake flickered through her brain. The way he'd looked at her, his blue eyes soft and filled with longing. His arms around her, strong and steady.

She swallowed, then drew in an unsteady breath, forcing herself to be pragmatic. Truth was, she'd let her feelings for Blake get out of hand. Let herself get closer to him than she'd intended. Come to care for him in a way she never wanted.

Falling in love with him would be easy. That was a no-brainer. All it would take was one more day with him, one more look from him, one more embrace, one more kiss.

She couldn't let that happen. She had to go to LA. She'd be living her dream as a designer while making sure her heart and happiness weren't dependent on a man. No question she was going.

She only hoped saying goodbye to Blake and Peyton wasn't a huge mistake.

Chapter Fourteen

Blake hung up his desk phone, equal parts of anxiety and happiness coursing through him.

His lawyer, Sharon Miller, had just called to tell him that the custody hearing had been moved up to the day after tomorrow due to a cancellation in the judge's schedule.

While Blake was ecstatic the whole custody process was moving forward quickly, he was also very apprehensive about the outcome. Very soon he'd be facing reality regarding Peyton's custody, and that fact had little needles of concern jabbing him. He could lose her within a matter of days.

Just what he needed when he was already tied up in knots about what had happened between him and Lily at the dance. As he'd lain awake last night, reliving every moment of that slow dance—how wonderful and happy he felt, every nuance of the song and how it related to him, the smell of her hair—he'd had no choice but to admit he was in grave danger of falling for Lily. Not what he'd wanted, or planned, but there you had it.

And now here he was, in the here and now, and he had some clarity. He wasn't going to lie to himself. Not about something this important.

The question was, what was he going to do about his dilemma? Did he jump in, headfirst, and admit his feelings to her? That seemed a bit reckless given so much was still up in the air. Actually, everything was still up in the air. Relinquishing control of his heart wasn't something to be done on a whim. He needed to be careful. Deliberate. Thoughtful. And sure of where he would ultimately end up. If that were even possible. Another rub.

His other option was to hold back and see what happened. After all, she wasn't leaving town for a while, and a lot could change in four months. That seemed like the more cautious way to go.

He'd finally drifted off to sleep from sheer exhaustion, with no clear plan in mind. Thankfully he still had plenty of time to decide what to do. Plenty of time to feel his way and work up his gut. Or not.

In the meantime, he hoped she was still willing to attend the hearing with him. He really wanted her there. Her levelheaded approach to life always kept him on an even keel, and if there was anything he was going to need when he went up against Mrs. Van Meter it was Lily's steady reliability.

An hour later, just as he was about to go out and work the front counter so Jonah could go to lunch, a knock sounded on his office door.

"Come in," he called.

The door opened and Lily stood on the other side, an umbrella clutched in one hand.

His senses jumped in excitement. It seemed as if he hadn't seen her pretty face in days, though in actuality it had been just last night. "Hey!" He stood, surprised to find his legs a little rubbery. "What brings you here?"

She hesitated on the threshold. "Well." She smiled. "I have some good news."

Though she'd said "good" news, an odd emptiness formed in his chest. Trying to ignore the sensation, he said, "Come on in."

The scent of an ocean breeze wafted to him as she came into the small office. She closed the door.

"Have a seat."

She sat, setting the umbrella on the floor at her feet.

When he was back sitting down, he folded his hands in front of himself on his desk, trying to look calm, cool and collected, even though anticipation bathed in anxiety curled in his gut. "So, what's this good news?"

Instead of replying she got to her feet. "I'm a bit warm. Let me get this coat off." She unzipped her hooded rain jacket and draped it over the back of the chair.

He sat patiently until she was settled again.

"So, last night after I got home from the dance, I got a call." She grinned. "It was a producer from *Project Fashion.*"

The hollow space in Blake's chest expanded. "Oh, wow. Why did they call?"

"That's the best part," she said, leaning forward, her eyes alight with enthusiasm. "Someone dropped out of the current competition at the last minute, and they want me to come down and take their place!"

Her elation was evident on her face. And rightly so. This was something she'd wanted for a long time. "Hey, that's great!" he said, infusing gusto into his tone. He wouldn't begrudge her this victory; deep down he wanted what was best for her, and this was it. "Congratulations."

"Thanks." She pressed her hands to her face. "It's all been such a whirlwind. I had to fill out paperwork and send it this morning, and I have to go shopping for travel stuff and I have to pack. There's so much to do."

This was really happening. She was going to LA for bigger and better things. Soon, not in a few months as he'd thought, as he'd been counting on.

A sinking sensation engulfed him, but he fought the swirling vortex of despair coming to life inside of him, determined to focus on the excitement of the moment for her sake. The last thing he wanted to do was be a downer. This was a big deal for her. And for him, but on the other end of the happiness spectrum.

"Um, when do you leave?" he asked, amazing himself by how normal he sounded. Good. He wouldn't for one second have her think he wasn't thrilled for her.

"My mom is driving me to Seattle the day after tomorrow," she replied. "My flight leaves that afternoon."

His breathing went ragged. *The day after tomorrow.* The day of the rescheduled custody hearing.

But…she didn't know that. And he wasn't telling her. He had to think of her at this moment, and he didn't want to mess up her plans with news of the moved-up appointment time. Knowing Lily, she'd turn her life upside down to be at the hearing—that was just the way she operated, always thinking of others—and he didn't want anything standing in the way of her getting to LA on schedule.

He put on a smile. "Oh, wow, when you said right away, you meant it." He'd been hoping for another week with her still in town at least. But he barely had a day.

"Yeah, it's fast, but I actually think it's better that way. Less time to worry, you know."

"You have nothing to worry about. I've seen your work. You're going to kill it down there." He truly believed that. "This is your time."

"I hope so," she said. "And don't worry. I've already decided I'll come back for the custody hearing." The one she thought was scheduled for late March.

"I never doubted you would," he said truthfully. She was one of the most giving people he'd ever known.

"That means a lot coming from you," she said quietly, giving him a soft smile that made his heart go mushy. "I'm going to miss you guys a lot."

"We're going to miss you, too," he said, just barely managing to keep his voice from breaking. The mere thought of her leaving in two days had a yawning emptiness taking over deep inside, leaving him feeling empty. Lonely. As if his world were ending.

As if she had become part of his heart...

Out of nowhere, a dumbfounding realization hit him like a blast of hot coffee from one of the latte machines at the store: he was in love with Lily Rogers. Though he'd grown to care for her, and admired the bond she'd developed with Peyton, he hadn't planned to fall *in love*. But that he loved her was undeniable. She would always have his heart.

Even if he never saw her again.

His shoulders sagged as his chest crumbled.

"Blake?" She leaned forward, her brow creased with concern. "What's wrong?"

"Hmm?" He made himself sit up straight, to appear as if nothing was wrong. "Oh, nothing." He looked around, and his gaze fell on some custody paperwork on his desk. "I, um, was working on some custody stuff, and it has me kind of preoccupied." True enough. He'd thought of little else—save Lily—ever since Mrs. Van Meter had come to see him.

"You sure?" Lily asked, peering at him, her eyes narrowed. "You seem...not yourself."

"Oh, sorry." He made a show of yawning. "I didn't sleep very well last night." And he hadn't. "That must be it."

"Did Peyton keep you up?"

"No, I just had a hard time turning my brain off." From thoughts of Lily.

"I get that," she said. "I had a hard time sleeping last night, too."

"Nervous excitement?"

"Yeah, mainly."

"What's the other part?" he asked with bated breath. Did he dare hope thoughts of him had kept her awake? Should he even let himself go there? Probably not.

She chewed on her lower lip. "I'm not sure there's any point in saying anything."

That intrigued him. "What do you mean?"

Unwinding the floral print scarf around her neck, she sat back. "I shouldn't have run away from you last night."

"So you *were* running away," he stated.

She cringed. "I was."

"Because?"

"Because that slow dance scared me," she said, her voice so soft he barely heard her. Even so, her words landed like an explosion. What did this all mean?

Unsure of where the conversation was going, he simply said, "Me, too." The truth of his feelings for her hovered in the back of his throat, but he held back, not wanting to add to the conflict obviously going on inside of her.

She sat for a silent moment. "I guess we should talk about what happened."

"That sounds like a great idea," he said. But then something occurred to him. "But…I hate to even say this…" He trailed off.

"What?" she said.

"Well…what's the sense in getting into the nuts and bolts of…all of this if you're going to leave anyway?"

She flinched. "Ouch."

Regret burned through him but he set it aside. He was talking about his life and his heart here; he had to be sensible. "Now isn't the time to pull punches."

She thought about that for a moment. "You're right."

He forced himself to say, "So, no matter what is said here, you're going to LA day after tomorrow." He leveled a direct stare on her. "Right?"

"I have to go—"

"You don't have to justify what you want to me." He loved her enough to let her go. Not that he could say that.

A visible shuddering breath moved through her. "I want to tell you why I'm going. I owe you that."

"Okay. Go ahead." If she needed to say it,

he'd listen. Whatever was necessary to make sure she followed her heart.

"My dream is right in front of me, there for the taking. I would never forgive myself if I didn't take advantage of this opportunity." She reached out across his desk and placed her hand on his. "The timing is bad, I know. And in another time and place, maybe my decision would be different. But now? Now I have to do this." She looked at him sideways. "I even prayed about it."

"You did?"

"Yep. It was so…comforting to have God help me with this decision." She looked Blake right in the eyes. "You showed me that."

"I'm glad you've reconnected with Him." Blake fought the urge to grip her hand and never let her go. "Even if you said you'd stay, I'd tell you to go."

"You would?"

He simply nodded.

"Why?"

"As I've said before, this is God's plan for you. Simple as that."

She was silent for a second, clearly thinking about what he'd said. Her hand squeezed his, and then she pulled away. "Thank you for understanding."

I'd do anything for you. "Your dream should

come true, no matter what." He wouldn't stand in her way.

No matter how much he loved her.

She needed no ties, nothing holding her back. She had to leave town and find what she'd always wanted.

And that wasn't him and never would be.

"I still can't believe the difference that hairstyle makes," Lily said from the passenger seat of Mom's car. Mom had had almost a foot cut off yesterday, and had colored the gray out. The new do fell in attractive waves to just past her shoulders, and took a good ten years off Mom.

Mom's new look was a welcome distraction from the knot of apprehension that had taken up residence in Lily's tummy—nerves on the loose—but she was doing her best to ignore the uncomfortable sensation and get herself on that flight to LA. Yes, the big day had arrived, and they were an hour outside of Moonlight Cove, well on their way to Seattle.

"I'm still not used to it," Mom said, glancing in the rearview mirror. "I'm almost afraid to touch it."

"You sure there's nothing going on I need to know about?" Lily said. Mom had come home last night with the cut, style and color, saying she just needed a change. But Lily sensed something else at the root of the new style.

"Well...Lionel Shaver asked me out again the other day, and I decided you were right."

"About what?"

"Oh, you know." Mom waved a hand in the air. "When you told me I was hiding behind my frumpy clothes and hair."

"I didn't say *frumpy*."

"I know, that was my word. But you were right. I was hiding behind that stuff, and for what? So I can live the rest of my life alone?"

A chill spread through Lily.

Mom continued on. "Your sisters will be out of the house soon enough, and then I'll be by myself, an empty nester. I need to build some kind of social life up, right?"

"Right," Lily said, surprised by her mom's turnaround.

"I can't believe I spent so many years running away from any kind of commitment." Mom paused. "I mean, I understand why I did it. I was scared. I only wish I had seen the truth sooner."

Lily furrowed her brow. "What brought all of this on?"

"I'm taking charge of my life, like you are.

You're going after your dream and aren't afraid of what you might be leaving behind."

Lily jerked in her chin. "What do you mean what I'm leaving behind?"

Mom gave her a pointed look. "Blake and Peyton, of course."

A knot of apprehension formed in Lily's throat. Words stuck in her mouth.

Mom continued, "As long as we're on the subject, would you like to share with me how you *do* feel about Blake?"

"I...like him." It was more than that, though. A lot more. Lily had known that for a long time. She'd just been good at hiding it. Or thought she'd been.

"Are you being completely honest, honey?"

Lily pressed her lips together. "I don't want to talk about this." Not when she was so close to making her escape.

Mom was significantly silent for a moment. "Why is that?"

With a jerk on her suddenly snug seat belt, Lily shifted in her seat, her jaw tight. "Why are you asking me all of this? You were the one who told me to follow my dream, if you remember, to focus on the prize. Why do you think I'm leaving something behind?"

"I did say that. You're right. But that was before I realized how you felt about Blake."

Uneasiness sank teeth into Lily. "I already told you I like him. Why do you think there's more?"

"I can just tell," Mom said softly. "I've been in love before. I know what it looks like."

Lily didn't know what to say, so she just sat there, shaking her head.

"So *have* you fallen in love with him?"

Something cracked open inside of Lily and she finally gave in. "I think I have. But I don't want to be in love with him."

"Sometimes the heart wants what it wants."

"Molly said essentially the same thing."

"Well, there you go," Mom said. "Two wise women can't be wrong."

Conflict warred within Lily. Maybe she needed to talk this out. "I'm scared of loving him, Mom, of giving up my dream for something so uncertain. Something that could hurt me in the end."

"Love is scary," Mom said. "Trust me, I know that. But it's also worth the risk." Her voice broke. "I know that from loving your dad. I wouldn't have traded that for anything."

"But you gave up your career as an artist for him. His death almost destroyed you."

Mom looked at her. "Yes, it almost did. But I still wouldn't trade the love we shared. And no, I didn't give up my career for him. I merely set it aside temporarily for myself and what my heart wanted."

"Temporarily?"

Mom smiled. "I put a portfolio together, and a gallery in Long Beach is interested in a few pieces."

"Oh, wow, Mom! That's fantastic!"

"Thanks. I'm pretty happy about it. But I'm scared, too. It's a step into the unknown, and that's always a risk. But my happiness is at stake." She turned a pointed stare to Lily. "What about *your* happiness?"

Lily closed her eyes and shook her head. "I thought I had this all figured out."

"Can you tell me you haven't had one moment of second thoughts?"

"No," Lily whispered, her struggle spiraling around in her like a whirlwind gone off the rails.

"Then you need to let yourself have those second thoughts and really think about what you're giving up right now." Mom turned off the radio. "One more question."

"Go ahead."

"Are you running *to Project Fashion*, or *away* from Blake?"

With the situation put in those explicit terms, Lily had no choice but to let her mind go to that forbidden place. The wonderful one where she was tucked safe in Blake's arms, with Peyton nestled between them, love flowing around, warm and wonderful and forever.

She turned. "What if he doesn't love me? What if I give LA up and I find out Blake doesn't return my feelings? How can I possibly set myself up for that kind of heartbreak?"

"What if you find out he does love you?" Mom said with a gentle glance before she returned her gaze to the road ahead.

Struck speechless by Mom's wise words, Lily sagged back in her seat, her breath whooshing out of her.

What if Blake loved her and she ran away and never knew it?

Horror spread through her and the last piece of the puzzle fell into place. If Blake loved her... A warm glow spread through her. If a wonderful, perfect, extraordinary man like Blake loved her, she would be the happiest woman in the world.

That thought made everything clear, and she wondered what the problem had been all along. How had she ever thought she could leave them behind? How could she actually run away from love? She couldn't. And hadn't she discovered that she could work and have other things in her life, at the same time? She'd worked on Josie's dresses and taken care of

Peyton while still keeping her commitment to Molly and helping with the Valentine's Day dance. She'd faced down multiple challenges, and it had all turned out fine. She'd succeeded.

She could do all of it. She knew that now.

"Mom, you're not going to believe this."

Mom put on her signal and guided the car to the side of the road. "Oh, I think I'll believe it."

"Turn the car around."

"Are you sure?" Mom said, hitting Lily with a solemn stare.

"Absolutely positive." With her pulse going haywire, Lily sat forward in her seat while Mom waited for a few vehicles to go by and then wheeled the car around and headed back the way they'd come.

Back to the man and the little girl who completed Lily.

She prayed the truth hadn't been too long coming.

With his lawyer, Sharon, by his side, Blake sat on a bench in a hallway at the Pacific County Courthouse, waiting to see the judge for the preliminary custody hearing. The hearing ahead of his had run late, and he and Sharon had been told that it would be at least half an hour until they'd see the judge.

Blake had spotted Mrs. Van Meter waiting

with her lawyer on his way in, and Blake had pointedly kept his focus away from her. Nothing good in letting her get to him any more than she already had. He wouldn't give her that power.

He was tempted to loosen his tie, but resisted the urge. Instead he leaned his forearms on his knees, his hands clasped together, his eyes on the floor, trying desperately to focus on the important matter at hand and keep Lily from his thoughts.

No easy task. He'd been in a major funk since she'd left his office the day before yesterday, full of excitement for her move to LA. While it did his heart good to see things going the way she wanted, it was still a blow to watch her walk out of his life.

But he still stood by his decision not to possibly sway her with declarations of love and any hints that the hearing had been moved up. He was firm in his resolve not to throw any roadblocks in her way.

He loved her too much to do that.

That thought had the ache in his chest expanding until breathing was hard.

How long would this pain last? Would he ever come to grips with losing Lily?

He cast his gaze upward, a prayer forming in his mind. *Lord, please keep Peyton in my life. I love her so much, and losing her, too, would be more than I could bear.*

Just as he was about to finally give in and loosen his tie, he heard quick footsteps echoing through the hallway. Lifting his head, he turned.

And saw Lily hurrying toward him, her hair flying out behind her, her eyes filled with obvious strain.

As shock barreled through him, he jerked to his feet. "Lily!" he said. "What are you doing here?"

Breathing hard, she put a hand on his arm. "I need to talk to you."

"Is something wrong?" he asked, looking her over quickly. Something bad must have happened if she were here rather than waiting at the gate at Sea-Tac.

Lily looked directly at him. "No, nothing's wrong." She leaned in. "Can we go somewhere more private?"

As more surprise jolted through him, he sensed Sharon getting to her feet beside him.

She said, "Go ahead, but stay close in case they call us early."

"Okay, thanks." Taking Lily's arm, he led her around the corner to stand next to a potted plant. The hall ended here, and was out of sight from anybody.

Shoving a hand through his hair, he turned to Lily.

Before he could speak, she said, "Why didn't you tell me the hearing was moved up to today?"

"Because I knew you'd find a way to stay, and I didn't want anything to keep you from going to LA." True, though it didn't tell the whole story.

"I don't know whether to be touched or mad." She gave him a scolding stare. "I wanted to be here for you for the hearing."

"Believe me, I love that it meant that much to you, but I know how long you've waited for the LA opportunity. You didn't need anything keeping you from being on that flight."

Her face relaxed. "I'll go with being touched, then," she said, pressing her free hand to her chest. "Putting me first was a very unselfish thing to do."

"I had a good role model," he said, meaning her. "You would have done the same thing." In fact, it looked as if she had done her own altruistic thing by returning to town, but he didn't want to assume anything. "Shouldn't you be at the airport right about now?"

"That was the plan," she said cryptically.

"What happened?" Why was she back?

"My mom and I were halfway to Seattle, and I realized that I couldn't leave."

"Why?" he asked, hope rising inside of him all over again.

She closed her eyes and shook her head. "I've been a complete idiot."

"What are you talking about?"

"I was running away again."

"From what?" The question burned its way through his brain. Was it possible she'd come back for him?

"Blake?" Sharon came around the corner. She waved a hand. "Judge McMillan is ready for us."

Apprehension cut a jagged path through him. "Okay."

Lily put a hand on his arm. "Everything is going to be all right," she said.

"What if it's not?" he said, unable to keep his pessimistic thoughts at bay.

"We'll get through it." Her eyes met his. "Together."

Together. Questions rolled around in his mind. What did that mean? Why had she come back? For him? For Peyton? Both? Or was she here as just a friend? Did he dare ask God for her love?

"Blake?" Sharon said urgently.

The questions would have to wait. "Coming."

"Go," Lily said. "I'll stay."

"Okay." Just the thought of having her here after the hearing had some of his tension easing. Without thinking, he pulled her into a hug. "Thank you for coming back."

She nodded and squeezed him tight. "I'll pray for you."

He forcibly pulled away from Lily, deeply touched. "Thank you." He turned and followed Sharon around the corner and up the hall to the door that would lead him to the person who would decide Peyton's future.

And Blake's, too.

And then the only question remaining would be whether Lily would be a part of that future, too.

Sitting on the hard bench in the hall outside the hearing room, Lily prayed as she'd never prayed before.

An hour later, with her entreaty to God sent up, her last nerve died a noisy death. Between stressing about the judge's decision and worrying about telling Blake she loved him, she was just about ready to come unglued.

When she'd told Mom to turn around, Lily had expected to find Blake at the store. So Mom had driven her straight to The Cabana. Lily had been disappointed and perplexed to find Blake gone and Jonah in charge. Jonah had told her that Blake had taken the afternoon off for some kind of "custody thing."

Her heart had just about collapsed. Custody hearing? Today? Okay, on to plan B. She'd called Blake's cell. Three times. No answer. Jim was next on the list. After a quick call to him, he confirmed Blake was at the county courthouse in South Bend, and that the hearing was scheduled for one o'clock, in just half an hour's time. Mom had broken every speed limit to get Lily to the courthouse, which was twenty miles from Moonlight Cove, before the hearing started.

And here she was, waiting, waiting, waiting, feeling as if her whole future hung in the balance. The day held the possibility of a triple whammy—she'd lost her chance to be on the show, Blake could lose custody and he might not return Lily's feelings. What would she do then? How would she deal with that possibility?

God, I haven't asked for much until today, but please, please, please help me deal with whatever happens between me and Blake with grace and strength. Amen.

She sucked in a large steadying breath, and then popped to her feet. Pace. She needed to pace.

Just as she finished the umpteenth circuit back and forth on the marble floors, she heard the hearing room door open.

She whipped around.

A tall, imperious-looking woman dressed in a suit that had to cost in the thousands walked out. Her bright red lips pressed into a scowl had wrinkles forming around her mouth and eyes.

Had to be Rich's mom. She looked unhappy. Livid, actually. Good sign?

With her heart hammering, Lily let the woman and a tall skinny man, presumably her lawyer, pass. Then Lily stepped forward, hoping with everything in her that the hearing had gone Blake's way.

Just as she reached to open the door, he stepped out into the hallway. When he saw Lily, his mouth broke into a huge grin.

The joy on his face had most of her tension draining out, as if someone had opened a floodgate inside of her. "What happened?" she asked.

"The judge reviewed all of the paperwork, asked some questions and then decided that there was no reason to change the custody situation." If possible, his grin became even bigger. "He awarded me full custody pending the rest of the legal process and paperwork."

She threw her arms around his neck and hugged him. "Oh, Blake, that's wonderful news!"

He enfolded her in his arms. "Yes, it is. It's perfect."

"You deserve this," she said, pulling back to look at him.

Sharon came out of the hearing room.

Blake dropped his arms and then turned. He held out a hand to Sharon. "Thank you," he said.

"You're welcome," she said, smiling as she took his hand. "I'll coordinate the paperwork and let you know what you need to do."

"Okay, that would be great."

She waved goodbye and left, her heels echoing on the floor as she headed to the double doors leading to the street.

Blake let out an audible sigh of relief. "Whew. So glad to have that over."

"You can relax now," Lily said, realizing the time to confess her love was at hand. Her tummy pitched.

"I think you and I still have some things to discuss."

She nodded solemnly. Big, life-changing things.

His gaze wandered to the windows behind her. "Let's go outside."

"Lead the way," she said.

Taking her hand, he started walking to the exit at the front of the building.

Within minutes they were on the sidewalk in downtown South Bend. Thankfully, the clouds overhead were broken up a bit by hints of bluish sky and patches of weak sun. She walked by his side, silent, not quite sure how to tell him what she had to tell him. Her courage faded with every step she took.

Finally, he stopped next to a Mexican café, which smelled like tortillas and salsa. He turned and hit her with his beautiful sky-blue gaze. "What's going on?"

"So." She gathered herself, striving for bravery. "You asked me why I came back."

"Yes, I did." He roamed his gaze over her face. "Why did you?"

The thought of losing Blake and Peyton forever gave her the mettle to put her heart on the line, to take the final risk to find everlasting happiness with Blake. "You," she whispered, grabbing his hand in her trembling one. "I came back because of you."

His jaw went visibly slack. "Me?"

She brought her other hand up to grip his tightly. "On the way to the airport, my mom asked me if I was running to *Project Fashion*, or away from you."

"What was your answer?"

"I told her I was running because I was scared of letting myself love you."

"So loving me is a possibility?" he said, his voice husky.

She felt her lips tremble. "It's not a possibility."

"It's not?" His words were barely a whisper.

"No, it's a reality." She let go of his hand and touched his cheek. "I'm already in love with you."

"So…you love me?"

She nodded. "Yes, I do. After seeing what my mom went through after she lost my dad, letting myself love you and maybe lose you frightened me. But I've realized that never taking the chance on us scared me more."

"But what about *Project Fashion*? That's always been your dream."

"Yes, it has. But I've learned that my happiness comes from designing, not from a show, and that I can pursue my career goals and still have a future with a family. My life doesn't need to be either/or." She sucked in a large breath, ready to take the plunge. "And I had to take the risk and tell you, had to put my heart on the line, or I knew I'd regret it for the rest of my life."

He pulled her into his arms and buried his lips near her ear. "I'm so glad you took the risk," he whispered huskily. "The reason I didn't tell you about the hearing was because I love you too much to stand in your way."

She pulled back just a bit. "So you did it because you love me?" Her voice shook and her eyes burned with tears.

"I didn't want to do anything that might influence your decision." He pressed his forehead to hers. "And I have to admit, I was scared, too."

"Love is terrifying," she said. "I almost bolted."

"But you didn't," he said. "That's what matters, right?"

"Right." She stepped back, still holding his hand. "I want to be a designer, no question, but I also want you in my life. I want both, and I know now that's possible."

"I love you, Lily Rogers, with my whole heart and soul. Please say you'll never run away again."

She smiled so big her cheeks ached. "Never again," she said. "You're stuck with me."

"And you're stuck with me," he said before he kissed her.

Breathing in his scent, she was content at last, secure in her love for Blake and in his for her.

Forever.

Epilogue

With a spring in her step, Lily let herself into Blake's house, excited to tell him how her meeting with Jean, her former boss at The Clothes Horse, had gone.

As Lily took off her coat and hung it in the closet by the front door, the smell of scented candles wafted her way. Puzzled, she headed into the kitchen.

Her breath caught. Blake stood by the table, a bouquet of gorgeous pink roses in his hand. He'd dimmed the lights, and several candles burned on the counter and on the table, which was decked out in a linen tablecloth and what looked like fine china and flatware.

"Oh, my." She smiled. "What's going on?"

"Happy Valentine's Day." He held out the flowers. "For you."

"For me?" she breathed as she took the bouquet from him. She'd never received flowers from a man. Burying her nose in the blossoms, she inhaled their sweet scent. "Wow. These smell wonderful."

"I know pink is your favorite color."

What a thoughtful guy. "Yes, it is." She craned her head, noticing that a complete dinner sat at the ready on the counter. "Valentine's Day was months ago."

"I know," he said. "But we missed it as a couple, so I decided to just celebrate it tonight."

For about the millionth time since that day in the courthouse her heart melted into a puddle of goo inside of her. "You've proven yourself to be a really romantic guy."

He shrugged. "Only for the right woman."

She was thrilled she was the right woman. She loved him so much, her heart was so full, so complete. A thought occurred to her. She cast her gaze around. "Where's Peyton?"

"I told her I wanted to be alone with the woman I love, and Peyton obliged and went to sleep early."

"She did?" Lily asked with a sideways look.

He grinned. "No, Jim and Fran took her for the evening."

A ribbon of excitement winged through Lily. "So it's just you and me?"

"Just us," he said, wagging his eyebrows. "And I cooked."

"You made this dinner?" Blake was a lot of things—wonderful things—but a good cook wasn't one of them.

"Well, I had a bit of help from Jim, but for the most part, yes, I made it." Blake gestured to her chair with a flourish. "Have a seat."

Once she was settled, he served her steak, potatoes and vegetables that looked as if they came from an expensive restaurant. He then poured them both some sparkling cider and sat beside her.

She raised her glass of cider. "To us."

"To us," he said, clinking her glass.

Goodness how she loved the sound of *us*. "To you and me."

After he took a drink, he asked, "So, how did your appointment with Jean go?"

More exhilaration fluttered through Lily. "She said she'd love to give me a reference to the community college design program."

"That's great!" he said. "What did she think of your idea to design baby clothes and sell them online?"

"She thought it was a fantastic idea, and she told me she'd also be interested in a silent partnership when I open a brick-and-mortar store on Main Street down the line."

He raised his glass again. "She knows talent when she sees it." He took a sip of cider and then said, "Are you sure you're all right with being eliminated from the show so early?"

Although she'd declared the show wasn't important to her, Blake had insisted she turn right back around and get on a flight to LA, telling her she shouldn't pass up the opportunity. Lily had hated to leave her new loves, but she'd realized he was right, and that the show's producers would be waiting for her, no matter what. Luckily the airline hadn't charged her to take a later flight, and Lily had reluctantly left Blake and Peyton with promises to call every day. She'd hated being away from them.

"I'm sure. I'm glad I did it. It was a great experience, I made some new contacts and I followed my dream. What is there to regret?"

"Absolutely nothing," he said. "Their loss."

His praise had warmth spreading through her. "Thanks." She took a sip of cider, wrinkling her nose when the bubbles hit. "I have more good news."

"What?"

"All of the dresses are done and fitted. Josie is thrilled." Lily had worked long hours after she'd returned from LA to finish the designs. The gowns, Josie's in particular, were some of Lily's best work, if she did say so herself.

"I knew she would be. The dresses were very pretty."

"They did turn out well, didn't they?" She grinned. "I love what I do."

He grinned back. "It shows."

"How did it go at the store today?"

"It was good."

"Any regrets?"

"About selling the store?"

She nodded. She'd been worried that he would look back and wish he'd somehow been able to pay the lawyer without selling The Cabana.

"Nope. I still get to run it day to day, but I don't have the stress of owning it." He picked up his fork. "Peyton was worth it, many times over."

"I'm so glad you see it that way." Lily picked up her fork and knife and started cutting her steak. "Anything more from Sharon?" Sharon was working on pushing the necessary paperwork through the right channels to officially establish Blake's full legal custody of Peyton.

"Things are moving along as fast as possible, but there's a lot of red tape."

"But it's going to happen eventually, right?" she said, hope lacing every word.

"Right. Before long, Peyton will be my daughter legally." He smiled. "Wow."

"Your daughter." Lily shook her head, but she was beaming, too. "That is so cool."

"I know. I still can't believe it myself." He turned soft eyes her way. "A lot of things have happened lately that I can't believe."

"I know, for me, too." Blake. Peyton. Her new interest in designing baby clothes, prompted by looking over Peyton's wardrobe and deciding most of her clothes were blah.

He reached out and touched her hand. "Have I told you lately that I love you?"

She caressed his stubbly jaw, looking into his eyes, falling into them as she did every time he was near. "Why no, you haven't." She'd never get tired of hearing it.

"I love you with my whole heart, Lily."

"And I love you, Blake. Always."

"Always," he breathed.

As she lost herself in the words that made her heart sing and completed her in a way she'd never dreamed, he pulled away and dropped to one knee.

Her breath left her in a rush and she pressed a quivering hand to her chest. She mouthed, "What?"

His eyes met hers again, and as always, she felt as if she were drowning in a pool of deep love, meant solely for her. Her heart sighed in pure bliss.

"Lily, I want to grow old with you, and I never want to leave your side." With a hand she could see shaking, he reached into his pocket and pulled out a dark blue velvet box. He flipped open the lid. Inside was nestled a gold ring set with a round diamond. Simple but beautiful. Exactly what she would have chosen. "Will you make me the happiest man in the world and do me the honor of becoming my lifelong partner, my wife?"

Her response was instantaneous. "Yes!" she yelled, every cell in her body shaking with elation. "Yes, I will!"

Taking the ring from the box, he put it on her left ring finger. "It's gorgeous," she said, barely able to speak.

"It was Fran's aunt's wedding ring, passed to her for safekeeping. Fran insisted I give it to you."

"I love it." Smiling shakily, Lily gazed at the ring. "It's perfect."

"You're perfect," he said, pulling her to her feet.

"So are you," she said back.

"*We're* perfect." He bent his head and pressed his lips to her ear. "I can't wait to make you my wife…and Peyton's mother." And then he kissed his way across her cheek to her lips. Lily lost herself in his tender embrace and heartfelt kiss, and the idea of being a wife and mother. A sense of total contentment settled around her.

And she knew that she'd finally found what she'd been looking for, what would make her happy for the rest of her life. The Lord's plan, indeed.

Thank You, God, for making all *of my dreams come true.*

* * * * *

Dear Reader,

I am so glad you joined me in Moonlight Cove for Blake and Lily's story. Lily was a secondary character in Book One of the Moonlight Cove series, *Family to the Rescue*. From the moment my critique partners read about her, they wanted me to make her the heroine in her very own book. I think Blake turned out to be perfect for her, though neither one thought so at the beginning of the book. Blake also made an appearance in Book Three, *Her Small Town Sheriff*, and when I wrote about him and The Coffee Cabana back then, I knew he was just the man for Lily. Aren't you glad they found each other?

I really get a kick out of coming up with new characters as well as sprinkling recurring characters here and there. If you read a book and find a single man or woman making an appearance, chances are he or she will have their own book eventually. I love telling the stories of those who are reluctant to put their hearts on the line but end up falling in love anyway. There's nothing better than a heart-warming tale of a man and woman realizing they're made for each other. Please be sure to look for more books in the Moonlight Cove series in the future.

Blessings,
Lissa

LARGER-PRINT BOOKS!

GET 2 FREE
LARGER-PRINT NOVELS
PLUS 2 FREE
MYSTERY GIFTS

Love Inspired®
SUSPENSE
RIVETING INSPIRATIONAL ROMANCE

Larger-print novels are now available...

YES! Please send me 2 FREE LARGER-PRINT Love Inspired® Suspense novels and my 2 FREE mystery gifts (gifts are worth about $10). After receiving them, if I don't wish to receive any more books, I can return the shipping statement marked "cancel." If I don't cancel, I will receive 4 brand-new novels every month and be billed just $5.24 per book in the U.S. or $5.74 per book in Canada. That's a savings of at least 23% off the cover price. It's quite a bargain! Shipping and handling is just 50¢ per book in the U.S. and 75¢ per book in Canada.* I understand that accepting the 2 free books and gifts places me under no obligation to buy anything. I can always return a shipment and cancel at any time. Even if I never buy another book, the two free books and gifts are mine to keep forever.

110/310 IDN F5CC

Name	(PLEASE PRINT)
Address	Apt. #
City	State/Prov. Zip/Postal Code

Signature (if under 18, a parent or guardian must sign)

Mail to the **Harlequin® Reader Service:**
IN U.S.A.: P.O. Box 1867, Buffalo, NY 14240-1867
IN CANADA: P.O. Box 609, Fort Erie, Ontario L2A 5X3

**Are you a current subscriber to Love Inspired Suspense books
and want to receive the larger-print edition?
Call 1-800-873-8635 or visit www.ReaderService.com.**

* Terms and prices subject to change without notice. Prices do not include applicable taxes. Sales tax applicable in N.Y. Canadian residents will be charged applicable taxes. Offer not valid in Quebec. This offer is limited to one order per household. Not valid for current subscribers to Love Inspired Suspense larger-print books. All orders subject to credit approval. Credit or debit balances in a customer's account(s) may be offset by any other outstanding balance owed by or to the customer. Please allow 4 to 6 weeks for delivery. Offer available while quantities last.

Your Privacy—The Harlequin® Reader Service is committed to protecting your privacy. Our Privacy Policy is available online at www.ReaderService.com or upon request from the Harlequin Reader Service.

We make a portion of our mailing list available to reputable third parties that offer products we believe may interest you. If you prefer that we not exchange your name with third parties, or if you wish to clarify or modify your communication preferences, please visit us at www.ReaderService.com/consumerschoice or write to us at Harlequin Reader Service Preference Service, P.O. Box 9062, Buffalo, NY 14269. Include your complete name and address.

LISLPDIR13R

Reader Service.com

Manage your account online!

- Review your order history
- Manage your payments
- Update your address

> ### *We've designed the Harlequin® Reader Service website just for you.*

Enjoy all the features!

- Reader excerpts from any series
- Respond to mailings and special monthly offers
- Discover new series available to you
- Browse the Bonus Bucks catalog
- Share your feedback

Visit us at:

ReaderService.com